T0120934

Broken Highway

Broken Highway

S.D. Laux

authorHOUSE®

AuthorHouse™
1663 Liberty Drive
Bloomington, IN 47403
www.authorhouse.com
Phone: 833-262-8899

© *2022 S.D. Laux. All rights reserved.*

No part of this book may be reproduced, stored in a retrieval system, or transmitted by any means without the written permission of the author

Published by AuthorHouse   07/08/2022

ISBN: 978-1-6655-6443-4 (sc)
ISBN: 978-1-6655-6444-1 (e)

Library of Congress Control Number: 2022912746

Print information available on the last page.

Any people depicted in stock imagery provided by Getty Images are models, and such images are being used for illustrative purposes only.
Certain stock imagery © Getty Images.

This book is printed on acid-free paper.

Because of the dynamic nature of the Internet, any web addresses or links contained in this book may have changed since publication and may no longer be valid. The views expressed in this work are solely those of the author and do not necessarily reflect the views of the publisher, and the publisher hereby disclaims any responsibility for them.

Chapter 1

Jackson woke up to someone banging on his front door. "What the fuck?" he said as he crawled out of bed. Jackson Thomas was an ordinary man. He had thick, brown hair and blue-grey eyes and was of average height and medium build. He had just turned forty-five and was recently divorced from his wife of twenty-two years. He had identical twin boys, Jared and Josh, who were in their last year of college.

"It's me!" Randy said.

Jackson looked at his phone. "Oh shit," he said realizing he was running late for work. He opened the door, and Randy backed up a little with two coffees in hand. "I'm so sorry, man." Jackson said as he took a coffee from Randy.

"What are you doing?" Randy asked as he came in. "I thought you were going into work today. I told you I was picking you up!"

"I know, I know," Jackson said as he went into the bedroom to get dressed; there was no time for a shower.

"What's wrong with you, man? You gotta get your shit together," Randy said shaking his head.

The thing was that Jackson wasn't motivated anymore. He was divorced. His kids were grown. He felt old, useless. All he wanted to do was be left alone, but Randy, his best friend and supervisor, wouldn't let him.

When Jackson came out of the bedroom looking disheveled, Randy looked him up and down and said, "Come on, man! You really going to work looking like this?" He put his coffee down and took Jackson to the bathroom. "At least comb your hair and brush them teeth! Your breath smells like stale beer."

Jackson did as he was told and downed his coffee. "Come on. Let's go!"

Jackson never felt that he belonged anywhere and even in his marriage. He felt something was missing and even more when the boys left for college. He and his wife, Lauren, were strangers living in the same house. Finally, they had both concluded that it was over and that it had been for a while. He had worked at the same company for over fifteen years as a warehouse supervisor for a car parts distribution center. He was over his job as much as he was over his marriage, and he didn't want to do it anymore. He went into work for the rest of the week just going through the motions. He realized he needed out. He needed to shake the feeling he was having. He wasn't depressed or even sad; he just felt stuck and restless. He needed a change before he got too complacent and another ten years passed him by.

Later that day at work, Jackson approached Randy and asked, "Hey Randy, you want to meet me after work today at Harry's? We need to talk."

"Sure," Randy said as he looked up from his computer in his office. "I'll be there at five."

Jackson got there a little early and was on his second beer when Randy arrived. "You're late," Jackson said as Randy sat across from him.

"So, what's going on?" Randy asked. They ordered a couple more beers. "You hungry?"

"No. I'll eat later tonight."

The truth was that it was Friday, and Jackson would be drinking all weekend; he had no room for food.

"So, what did you want to talk to me about?" Randy asked.

Jackson just looked at him and without thinking too much about it said, "I quit."

"You what? How drunk are you, Jackson?"

Jackson laughed. "I'm done! I'm over that place. I need a change."

"Are you serious, man? You're really quitting?" Randy started getting a little upset. "I know you're going through some things right now, and I've tried to be there for you, but this is ridiculous. You're really going to quit?"

"Listen, Randy, I'm sorry, but if I don't do something different, I'll go insane."

"OK then, but what are you going to do? Binge drink your days away and not work?"

"I want to travel, to see our country. I don't know. Just do what I want to do when I want to do it!"

"What … like a truck driver?"

"Yes, a truck driver. That's exactly what I think I want to do." He was buzzing when he said it, but he realized that maybe it was his next chapter in life.

"OK, OK, I've heard enough," Randy said. "I gotta go. I'll talk to you tomorrow after you sober up." Randy got up and left Jackson there alone.

Jackson paid the bill and got up to leave. He lived just around the corner, so he walked home. He passed out the minute his head hit the pillow.

He woke up the next morning hungover. It was already past nine. As he was taking a shower, he realized that Randy was right, that he needed to pull himself together. Thoughts of what Randy had said about his being a truck driver came back to him. *Why not? I could do that!*

He trimmed his beard, dressed, and got on the phone. Randy had left him a few messages asking him to call him back. Then he saw a few messages from Lauren, his ex. She was telling him that there was an offer on the house.

He couldn't believe that this was his life now, that he wasn't married. Sure, he had wanted the divorce and maybe even more than she did but being married had been a big part of his life for so long. They had married right after college and had the twins soon after, so there really hadn't been that much of a newlywed stage. All their focus had been on the twins and Jackson's job. That's basically what he had done for twenty years. But at that point, his life was different. He was alone but had options.

He texted Lauren back: "That's great. What's next?"

"Let's meet later today at your apartment," she texted.

He really wasn't in the mood to see her. She had moved on and seemed happy with her life, her job, and a new relationship. She knew what she wanted. Jackson on the other hand was drinking his days away and was seriously thinking of quitting his job and becoming a truck driver. "Sure. Come on over," he texted.

"OK. I'm on my way."

Shit! he thought. He didn't think it would be that soon. He started cleaning his apartment, which consisted of him throwing things into the closet and kicking stuff under the bed. He was a mess and lived in one. He didn't want her to see it because she would judge him.

Lauren knocked on the door. They hadn't seen each other in over six months. Opening the door, he felt a little something when he saw her. She was pretty, and that day, she looked extra put together in an olive-green sundress and sandals with toenails painted a hot pink. For a minute, he thought she had dressed up because she was seeing him.

"Hi. How are you, Lauren?" he asked as she leaned up and kissed his cheek. The place looked empty. The blinds were closed.

"I don't have a lot of time. I'm meeting Marco for lunch," Lauren said as she sat at the kitchen table with papers in her hands. Jackson felt a little jealous that she had moved on so quickly.

"So, what did you want to talk about, Lauren?" Jackson asked suddenly feeling a little annoyed. Since he'd been drinking so much lately, he really didn't have patience for anything.

"Here," she said handing him the papers. "These are the papers about the sale of the house. I'm going to pay off the school loans for the boys so they won't have any debt. And I'm paying off that huge credit card bill we had together so we won't be in debt either. I'm going to split up the remaining thirty thousand, fifteen for you and fifteen for me."

Jackson didn't say anything. He was happy to get that much. And he trusted her a hundred percent. She was always honest and fair. After taking the papers, Jackson walked her to the door. He had mixed feelings when he saw her go. He felt sad that it was really over and that there was nothing keeping them connected except the boys, but he also felt relieved. He decided that he was really going to start getting himself together especially after seeing Lauren.

He texted Randy telling him that he was serious about quitting and that he'd give his two weeks' notice on Monday. Then he started looking up truck driving schools. While he searched, he got a text from Randy: "OK, I understand. If you're serious about being a truck driver, here's a link to the school my brother-in-law Keith went too. He said that it was a reasonable price and that they gave you a lot of time to get your license."

He was grateful for Randy's support. They had been friends for a long time as were their wives and kids. But ever since he started having marriage problems, their friendship changed along with Jackson's attitude and behavior. Randy was doing more babysitting him and covering for him more than anything, so his quitting would take a load off Randy's shoulders.

Jackson called the school and decided to go there the same day. He wanted to sign up before he talked himself out of it or started drinking for the day. He got in his pickup, which needed a wash, and drove to the trucking school. The school wasn't that big; only about four big trucks were there along with a trailer that read "Rashid Trucking School" on the door.

Jackson got out and looked around a little before going into the office. Sitting at a desk with just a laptop and a cup of coffee was a dark-skinned Indian man. He stood when he saw Jackson walk in; Jackson figured that he must have been only five-four.

"May I help you?" he asked in a thick Indian accent.

"Yes. I'm looking to sign up for truck driving school."

"OK, my brother. I'm Rashid, the owner and operator of this school and one of the instructors," he said holding out his hand. "You can sit here. I'll get the paperwork together."

Jackson signed up, paid Rashid $1,500, and went home, where he drank for the rest of the day. He woke up on the couch the next morning dehydrated and sore from having slept on the couch. *I really need to get myself together*, he thought as he went to take a shower. He was starting truck driving school on Tuesday, so he had to officially quit his job and sign papers on Monday. He decided to get his house in order and dry out. *Meaning no drinking tonight.*

He woke up on Monday feeling actually good about his decision. He wasn't hungover, and he had a bit more energy than he had had for weeks. He showered and donned blue Levi's with a button-up Ralph Lauren shirt and work boots he had bought the previous week. He wanted to look good that day.

When he pulled into the parking lot at work, he felt a little sad and nervous; this was a big step. His job had been a big part of his life for over fifteen years. Jackson went in and saw that everyone was looking at him, people he had known for a long time, friends of his.

"You're really doing this?" asked Oscar, one of Jackson's employees.

"Yeah, I am," Jackson said as he put his hand out for a handshake. "I need a change."

"I get you," Oscar said. "Sometimes, I feel the same way."

The two shook hands. Jackson liked Oscar. He was a good employee, a good man, a family man with three kids under the age of six and a mortgage. Jackson knew Oscar really needed his job; he planned on suggesting to Randy that Oscar was the best one to take his job.

"Good luck with everything," Oscar said. "And don't be a stranger. Let's keep in touch."

"Let's do that," Jackson said, but he knew he'd probably never hear from any of these people again.

"So, OK now," Randy said as Jackson came into his office. "Take a seat. Let's get this process started."

Jackson could tell that though Randy said that he understood and was supportive, he was upset about his leaving. He didn't blame Randy at all. He knew he'd been a pain in the ass for a while. They talked for a while, and Jackson agreed to work two weeks part time to get Oscar ready for the supervisor job; he would still be able to go to school after his four-hour shift.

The two weeks went by fast, and even though he couldn't be at school all day, he was still learning fast. On his third week, Rashid told him, "Hey, my brother. You're ready. I think it's time you take your test next week," he said.

"My test?" Jackson asked.

"Yes, for your class A license," Rashid said with a smile.

"You really think I'm ready?" Jackson asked. He was nervous but confident; he knew he was doing well.

"Yes, you're ready," Rashid said again.

A beat-up, red Honda Civic pulled into the driveway, and a young man about six foot tall got out of it. Jackson watched as he and Rashid talked a little and went into the office.

"Jackson!" Rashid yelled and waved Jackson into his office.

"What is it?" Jackson asked.

"I want you to meet Robert Cochran. He's gonna be my new student."

"Hello," Jackson said as he shook Robert's hand.

Robert, who couldn't have been older than twenty-five, had short, light-brown hair and light-blue eyes. He was lean, but Jackson noticed that he stayed in shape. His posture, the way he looked and acted, and the firm handshake told Jackson that he was in the military. "Are you an instructor?" Robert asked Jackson.

"No," Jackson said. "A student."

"My best student ever!" Rashid said. "He's a natural. Jackson, would you show Robert around while I make a couple of phone calls?"

Jackson felt put on the spot, but he also felt sorry for Rashid, who had been doing everything since his other instructors had quit. "Sure," Jackson said. "C'mon, man. Let me show you around. So, you were in the Marines?" Jackson asked as they headed to a truck.

"Is it that obvious?" Robert asked.

"Kinda," Jackson said. "That tattoo on your forearm kinda gave it away."

"Oh, yeah, right," Robert said. "I got it just before my second tour."

"Two tours? Wow! How old are you?"

"Twenty-five. I would have done a third tour, but I got some shrapnel in my leg at the end of my second tour."

"Wow!" Jackson said. "That must have been crazy!"

"Yeah, pretty much," said Robert. He wanted to change the subject. "So, is this what I'll be driving?" he asked pointing to the truck.

"Yes, but when you get an actual truck driver job, you'll be driving something way bigger."

Jackson had picked up on Robert's reluctance to talk any more about his time in the Marines, so he engaged him in just small talk and showing him the inside and outside of the rig.

"Let's take him for a ride," Rashid said as he walked up behind them. "Come on, Jackson," he said throwing Jackson the keys. "You can drive."

They spent an hour talking and driving, and Jackson liked Robert. He could tell he was a good kid, but he also could tell that he was going through a lot at such a young age.

The next day, Jackson woke up feeling good, motivated, and ready for the day. He took his test that day and got 100 percent on the written part as well as the driving part. He texted Randy with his good news and asked him if he wanted to go out that night to celebrate. He then went to the school to tell Rashid and saw Rashid and Robert just getting back. Robert was already in the driver's seat, and as he was backing up

8

S.D. Laux

the rig, Rashid was yelling at him in his thick accent, which struck Jackson as funny; he had to stop himself from laughing.

"Jackson!" Rashid said as he jumped out of the truck. Robert stayed in the truck for a while taking deep breaths and trying to calm down.

"I got it!" Jackson said waving his license.

"Good job, my brother!" Rashid said hugging Jackson and shaking his hand.

When Robert got out of the truck, Jackson asked, "How are you, Robert?" but he could tell by Robert's expression that he wasn't doing too well.

"I'm fine. Congrats on your license!"

Rashid got a phone call. He started talking in Hindu but then stopped and told Jackson and Robert, "I'm gonna take this call in my office. Robert, we're done for the day. I'll see you tomorrow. And Jackson, can you come by tomorrow and help me out till you find a job? I really need your help, and I'll pay you."

Before Robert or Jackson could reply, he was back on the phone and in his office.

"I don't know if I can do this, man," Robert said shaking his head, leaning against the rig.

Ever since he had finished physical therapy after getting out of the hospital, he hadn't known what to do with himself. He had enlisted in the Marines right after graduation and didn't really know anything else. He believed that he could still be a marine, but his injuries were too severe.

"Listen, Robert, you can do it. If I can, you can."

"I don't know. I drove a tank in Afghanistan, but driving this truck and having this man yelling at me, which I can barely understand, I feel like I'm just gonna fuck up."

Jackson saw the desperation in the kid's eyes; it made him think of his boys. "OK, I guess I got a job for a couple of weeks. I'll help you through it. Come by in the morning. Since I have my license, maybe Rashid will let me train you."

He invited Robert to meet him in a couple of hours at Harry's. Robert liked Jackson; he seemed like a cool older man, and he left feeling better. Jackson went into Rashid's office to confirm his temporary job.

"You can be full time if you like," Rashid said with a laugh.

"No. I'm looking to hit the road as soon as I can! But I'll help you out in the meantime, Rashid."

Jackson went home to change. He was excited about going out that night but was a little nervous about drinking too much. He was doing so well in other respects.

He arrived at Harry's a little early, sat at a table toward the back, and ordered some wings and a bottle of Bud Light. He was just finishing up his wings when Randy walked in and came over to him.

"Congrats, Jackson. You're looking good!" Randy said extending his hand to Jackson.

"Thanks!" Jackson said wiping his hand of barbecue sauce before taking Randy's hand.

The waitress came over and asked Randy, "What can I get you?"

"I'll take a shot of tequila and a Corona," Randy said.

"Tequila?" Jackson asked with a laugh. "Has your day been that bad?"

"Bad enough, but we're here not to talk about my day. We're here to celebrate your new career."

The waitress returned with his shot and beer. "Need a menu?"

"No, I'm good," Randy said, "but how about another shot? Jackson, you want one?"

"No, but I'll take another Bud Light."

The waitress left, and Jackson said, "I thought I was the one with the drinking problem."

"I just need to take the edge off," Randy said as he took the shot and a swig of beer.

Randy congratulated Jackson on his class A license, and they talked a bit.

Jackson looked over by the door hoping to see Robert but instead saw a heavyset man with a Rolling Stones T-shirt that was way too small for him staring at him; that made him uneasy. He hated being stared at. "What's this guy's deal?" Jackson asked Randy.

"What guy?" Randy asked feeling a little buzzed.

"That fat fucker over there," Jackson said.

"Oh my God. That's my brother-in-law, Keith, the truck driver I told you about. Hey Keith! Over here!" Randy yelled.

"Man, he's huge!" Jackson said as Keith started toward them.

"That's a typical truck driver's body. You'll be looking like that soon enough," Randy said with a laugh.

The two got up to greet Keith, and Randy said, "Keith, glad you could make it. This here's the guy I was telling you about, Jackson Thomas. He just got his class A license."

"Nice to meet you," Jackson said shaking Keith's calloused hand.

They sat, and Keith said, "So you're looking to be a trucker. Why so late in life? How old are you?"

"I'm forty-five, and I'm looking to do something different."

"I get it—a midlife crisis," Keith said with a laugh.

Already, Jackson didn't like him.

The waitress came for Keith's order, which was wings and fries and a large Dr Pepper. *No wonder he's so fat*, Jackson thought.

They talked about the life of a truck driver, but instead of listening, Jackson was distracted by the way the guy ate with his mouth open and licked his fingers; he was already on his second large Dr Pepper when he was telling Jackson about how alone he would be on the road.

"I know," Jackson said. "I'm divorced, and my sons are grown."

When someone yelled, "Jackson!" he looked up and saw Robert by the bar looking uncomfortable, out of place.

"Who's that kid?" Randy asked.

"My buddy from driving school," Jackson said as he went over to the bar to meet Robert.

"Hey, sorry I'm late. I had a meeting to go to."

"No problem. Come on, I'll introduce you."

Robert didn't like bars. He would start drinking, which wasn't good because he was on antidepressants. He didn't tell anyone about that; he just wanted to be normal, be around people who didn't know his whole history. It wasn't just his leg that had been injured in Afghanistan; it was also his mental health.

They talked for about an hour, and then Randy and Keith decided to leave. "My wife's gonna kill me if I miss dinner," Keith said as he got up to leave.

"Dinner?" Randy asked. "Didn't you just eat a whole pile of wings and three Dr Peppers?"

"Just a snack," Keith said, and they all laughed.

Jackson was happy to see them go. He was dying to go over to a little brunette who had been checking him out the whole time.

Robert wanted to talk to Jackson alone; he felt comfortable with him. "So that was interesting," he said.

"Hey, *umm*, I'm gonna get another beer. You want anything?" Jackson asked as he looked at the brunette.

Robert could tell that Jackson wanted to talk to the girl, and he didn't want to be a third wheel. "No, I'm good. I'm gonna bounce. I gotta get home too."

"OK, sure," Jackson said not even really looking at Robert, who was disappointed. Jackson wasn't thinking of anyone but himself and getting laid.

Chapter 2

Jackson woke up the next morning hungover and late. He was supposed to be at the school by 9:00 a.m., and it was 8:45 a.m. *Oh shit!* he thought as he pushed the covers off his naked body. He heard the shower running and remembered that he had brought that cute little brunette home.

He dressed in a hurry. He told Rashid and Robert that he would be there to help them out. He felt guilty and pretty shitty for the way he had treated Robert the previous night. He went into the bathroom to take a leak, wash his face, and brush his teeth.

The brunette poked her head out of the shower. "Hey, I'll be out in just a minute if you want in, or you can join me."

"No, I'm good. I'm actually late! I got somewhere I need to be, so can you hurry up so I can drop you off?"

"OK," she said. She turned off the shower and grabbed a towel hanging on a hook.

"Sorry to be rushing you, but like I said, I'm late," Jackson said as he tied his boots.

"Hey, by the way, my name's Emily if you were interested," she said as she got dressed.

"OK, Emily, you almost ready? We got to go!" Jackson felt bad for rushing her.

"Well, for what it's worth, I had a good time last night," Emily said as she wrote her number on a pad Jackson kept on the fridge. "Call me if you want to hook up again."

That was the last thing on Jackson's mind; all he wanted to do was get to the school.

He dropped her off about two blocks out of his way. "Can I get a goodbye kiss at least?" Emily asked. Jackson gave her a quick peck and watched her go into her apartment before he floored it all the way to the school. He was already over an hour late.

"Finally!" Rashid exclaimed as Jackson walked into the office. "I was just about to take Robert out on the road."

"I'm here! Sorry, guys, but my alarm didn't go off."

"That's OK. You're here now," Rashid said. "Make sure you take him on the freeway, OK?" Rashid said as he got up to get the truck keys.

Jackson and Robert walked out, and Jackson said, "Listen, Robert, I'm sorry about last night. I was a jerk to you."

"No worries, man," Robert said. "I get it. I wish I'd gone home with someone last night too."

"Yeah, well, I'm still sorry."

They didn't say any more about it as they got into the truck and took off toward the freeway.

"You sure I'm ready for the freeway?" Robert asked.

"Yes, more than ready."

For the next two weeks, Jackson trained Robert along with two other guys, but he spent more time with Robert. They talked about everything. He felt sorry for the kid and all the shit he had been through, so he did everything he could to encourage him and praise him.

Jackson also hooked up with Emily two more times. He liked her company; he always had a good time with her but nothing serious, which was how he wanted his sexual relationships to be.

He finally got an interview at the trucking company Keith worked for—FRD Trucking, whose initials stood for Fast Reliable Delivery. The interview was easy—just a few questions, a good driving record, high school diploma, and he got the job. He was beyond excited. He needed this. He was getting restless and discouraged, and he was drinking more.

"So, congrats!" Rashid said as Jackson came in for his last week.

"Thank you," Jackson said. "How did you find out?" He hadn't told anyone.

"They called me for a reference and wanted to know how you were in your training. I of course said only good things."

"Thank you so much, Rashid! You've been a good mentor and friend," Jackson said shaking Rashid's hand.

"I'm gonna miss you," Rashid said. "You sure you don't want to stay and work for me?" he asked with a laugh.

"I can give you till the end of this week, but then I'm off to Modesto for my new job."

At that point, Robert was passing his class A test, and Jackson made sure to give him the information about where he would be working so he could apply for a job there too. He knew Robert needed to work, needed something to do as much as he did.

FRD's yard was huge. Jackson had never seen so many big rigs in one place before. FRD was a huge company with many employees and lots of contracts. He felt a little intimidated and overwhelmed by the whole thing. He was assigned a mentor—of all people Keith, whom Jackson learned had requested to be his mentor. Jackson would learn the ropes from Keith for three weeks or so before he got his own truck and trailer.

"We meet again," Keith said as he shook Jackson's hand.

"Thanks for helping me get the job, man," Jackson said.

"No problem," Keith said. "You're good friends with my brother-in-law, and he had only good things to say about you. All you gotta do is listen, pay attention, and follow my lead. And in probably two days, you'll be driving this thing."

"Two days? Don't you think I'll need more than two days?" Jackson asked feeling the sweat on the back his neck; he was getting nervous.

"Hey, guy, I know you know how to drive, and the best and fastest way to learn is to jump on the horse," Keith said as he pointed to the truck.

The first day, Keith showed him all he needed to know about the truck—how to check tire pressure and put gas in it and what to look at on the gauges. This truck was so big and so different than what he was used to.

"OK, it's time to hit the road," Keith said as he got dispatched to their first location.

Jackson got into the passenger seat and took a deep breath, closed his eyes, and said a quick prayer. They were going to Washington State.

The drive was nice; Jackson saw beautiful trees and clear sky, and he felt something he hasn't felt in a while—peace and tranquility.

He paid attention to everything Keith did, and Keith was a good driver—actually, one of the best the company had. He had put in almost twenty years there and wanted to do at least five more, but he was becoming overweight and had high blood pressure; he was prediabetic, and he was becoming a liability for the company, so he needed to change.

"I'm gonna pull over at this truck stop and get something to eat. You must be hungry," he said to Jackson.

"Yes, I can eat," Jackson said, "and I'm dying for a little caffeine."

"Can I ask you for a favor?" Keith asked.

"Yeah, sure. What is it?"

"I need to go on a diet. I can see by looking at you that you keep in shape, and I believe we're about the same age. Can you help me get into better shape? Even if you have to knock food out of my hands," Keith said laughing.

Jackson couldn't believe what Keith was asking, but he felt for him; he knew it had taken a lot for him to ask him for his help. The truth was that Jackson had never had a weight problem; he ate in moderation and worked out but not too much. He had a very fast metabolism.

"Sure, OK," Jackson said. "You need to first cut out sugar and carbs and drink lots of water. And we can work out a bit at the rest stops. Walking's a really good workout."

The next couple of weeks went by quickly. Jackson loved driving; he would drive mostly nights and sleep during days, when Keith would drive. They ate only Weight Watcher dinners they got at Walmart and protein drinks or bars. Keith was determined to lose weight, and Jackson was determined to help him; he wanted to avoid getting overweight himself. It was hard to stay in shape when he was always sitting on his ass.

"You know, Jackson, you've been a really good protégé, and you're a good truck driver. You'll do really well on your own. And thanks a lot for helping me lose weight! I actually lost twenty pounds!"

"That's awesome!" Jackson said. "I can see it. Just make sure you keep it up. And Keith, you've been a good mentor. Thanks for everything, man."

It was their last day together. Jackson would be getting his own truck and trailer the next day, and that made him anxious and excited at the same time. On their way back to the distribution center, Keith was talking nonstop as if he were making up for lost time; they really hadn't talked much at all, at least not about personal stuff.

Keith told Jackson about his life as a trucker—all the good and bad things he'd done and been through. He talked about his family life and how he was on his second marriage, that his first marriage had fallen apart due to all the cheating he'd done on the road. Jackson didn't know if he should feel bad for Keith or scared for himself.

"So, tell me, Jack, what's the real reason you want to be a trucker?" Keith asked. He was the only one who called him Jack.

Jackson thought for a moment before answering. He tried to come up with a reason that would sound logical, but he finally decided just to be honest. "I really don't know," he said shaking his head. "I just felt drawn to it. I looked at it as an escape from my old life. Like you said, Keith, that night I met you—a midlife crisis. And so far," he said looking at the setting sun as they started coming back into California from Oregon, "I love it. I feel at peace. I don't know how to explain it."

"I get you," Keith said. "I've been driving for almost twenty years now, and I'm still amazed by our country."

The more Jackson talked with Keith, the more he liked him. He had gotten comfortable with him, and he had told Keith more about himself than he had anyone else, and he felt good that he was able to help him out with his diet.

They pulled into the distribution center after midnight; Jackson was driving. He was supposed to be up by eight the next morning, and he needed sleep. He parked the truck, undressed into his sweats and T-shirt, and climbed up on the top bunk. Keith was snoring away on the bottom bed of the sleeper. That was one thing he was looking forward to—having a bigger and more comfortable bed.

At seven the next morning, Jackson woke up to Keith moving around in the sleeper.

"Hey, sorry to wake you," Keith said, "but I need to get going this morning. I have a load I need to deliver in San Jose."

"That's OK," Jackson said as he jumped down from his bed. "I gotta get ready anyway. I'm meeting the boss man at nine and getting my own truck."

"Awesome!" Keith said.

Jackson gathered his laundry and was tying his boots when his cell rang. "Hello?" he answered. It was his boss reminding him that he was to be at his office at nine sharp, that he already had a load for him to pick up. "Shit, man, I already have my first load," he said feeling a little nervous.

"That's how it is," Keith said. "No time to really chill there on your ass, but you'll do good."

"Thanks a lot, Keith. I guess I'll be seeing you around." The two shook hands. "And keep up with the diet. You're looking good!"

"I will! I feel more energetic and less lazy and tired since I've been watching my weight. Hey, Jackson, if you have any questions or need my help, just call me. I'll always be your mentor."

Jackson went to the distribution center and took a shower, something he hadn't done in a few days. He also trimmed his beard. He put on his black Levi's and a button-up plaid shirt; he wanted to make a good impression. It would be the first time he'd meet and talk to the big boss man. After putting a load of laundry in the washer, he went to the office and saw a man who appeared to be in his sixties; he had thin and balding brown hair and a thin white beard. He was on the phone and looking at his computer when Jackson walked in. He looked up at Jackson. "Give me a minute. Take a seat."

Jackson sat opposite him for a good five minutes listening to him arguing with whoever was on the other end. *Oh shit*, Jackson thought.

The man got off the phone, looked again at his computer, and said, "So you're Jackson Thomas. OK, here you are. I'm Jim Hill. I'm the main guy around here."

The two talked for about fifteen minutes; Jim gave Jackson all the paperwork he needed for the truck he was going to drive and be responsible for.

"Listen," Jim said. "I know you're a good driver. I got only good reports from Keith, so all I'm gonna say is that you drive only the scheduled time and you take your breaks at the scheduled times, not earlier or later, you understand?"

Jackson nodded.

"And also absolutely no alcohol or drugs! You can have a beer or two on your days off but none while driving, understand?" Jim looked back at the computer. "Let's get you back on the road." He printed out a paper with his routes on it. "Any questions?" Jim asked handing the paper to Jackson.

"No, I'm good," Jackson said still taking in everything Jim had said.

"OK, now get out of here and back to work."

Jackson extended his hand, and Jim shook it; he had quite a grip for an older man. Jackson hadn't even left the office before Jim was back on the phone arguing with that same guy.

He finished his laundry and put everything in his duffel bag along with his blanket and pillow. He went to where they had said his truck was. It was a big eighteen-wheeler with a gold cab that said FRD Trucking Company on it, with a trailer already attached. It was love at first sight. The truck was beautiful and shiny and had just been washed. He looked twice at the number on the truck to make sure it was his.

The inside of the sleeper was pimped out with a fridge and microwave. When he opened the fridge, he saw waters and some Gatorades and a note: "Congrats! Drive safe! Your mentor, Keith." Jackson smiled. He inspected the truck, sat in the driver's seat, looked at his load sheet, put on in his navigation, started the truck, checked all his mirrors and gauges, and took off out of the driveway.

Chapter 3

It was a cool morning. The sun was bright, and the air felt good. Jackson was feeling relaxed and in control and free. His first stop was a Target in Lancaster, California, where he'll drop off his trailer, pick up another one in Mojave, and head to Las Vegas.

He knew he was a good driver. Even Keith had been impressed with how well he did. He was good at backing up, which saved a lot of time. He only dropped off the trailers; he didn't unload anything. He was a truck driver, and he was paid only to drive. On his way back from Mojave to Vegas there was traffic; it was a Friday, so most likely, many were going to Vegas for the weekend. He made sure he took his breaks, listened to the dispatch, and got his sleep.

On his free time, he washed his clothes, got his hair cut, and worked out. He had a routine, and the first couple of months went by quickly. He mainly did the same routes and went to the same truck stops. He started to get a bit lonely; he needed a woman's company, but he didn't want to go after any of the skanky lot lizards Keith had warned him about. They were prostitutes who hung out at truck stops.

One night, he got on the internet and checked out a few call girl websites. He was in Vegas, so it was legal. He had a thirty-four-hour reset, which means a mandatory rest period for all truck drivers, so he decided to get a room and call up a date. He took a long shower, ate something, and scheduled his date for eight that night. It was still early, so he closed the curtains, turned off the TV, and took a three-hour nap.

He woke up about six feeling rested and ready. He needed some female attention even if he had to pay for it. It had been a while since he'd even touched a woman.

At eight on the dot, he heard a knock on the door. He opened it and saw a cute little blonde in a pink blouse and black miniskirt. He just gazed at her for a good twenty seconds. He couldn't believe a call girl could look that good, and he was horny as hell.

"You're Jackson, right?" she asked.

"Yes, yes. Come in, come in."

He paid for the whole night, and though it was very satisfying, there was something missing in the intimacy, the closeness. He knew not to expect that from a call girl, but he didn't know what he really wanted. He still felt lonely, and he needed to actually talk to someone. He started getting homesick even though he didn't really have a home anymore. He was alone.

At the end of the week, he went back to the distribution center in Modesto. He was tired, worn out; the driving was getting to him. He needed a few days off. He was just unloading his bag from the truck when he saw someone he recognized. "Oh my God! Is that you, Robert?"

"Yes, it's me, man!"

"How ya doing?"

"Real good, Jackson. I finished my mentorship and will be starting my driving on Monday."

"Awesome! Who was your mentor?"

"Keith."

"He was mine too!"

"I know. Keith said you were a good protégé, and he's a good teacher."

"Is he keeping up the diet and exercise?"

"Yes sir. Believe me, I kept him in shape!"

They laughed and swapped stories about their time with Keith.

Robert looked at Jackson's truck. "I hope mine's as nice as yours."

"It should be, Robert. They're all basically the same except mine's a little newer. So what are you doing tonight?"

"Nothing really. You got something in mind?"

"Yeah. I have a few days off, and I really need to be around people I know. You want to hang out tonight?"

"Sure. Just text me when and where. I gotta go see the boss man."

"Good luck with that," Jackson said with a chuckle.

He was feeling better. He drove to his little, one-bedroom apartment, which he hasn't been to in over three months. He put his stuff down, opened a few windows, lay on his bed, and knocked out for the rest of the afternoon.

His phone woke him up. For a few seconds, he didn't know where he was. He reached for his cell. "Hello?"

"Dad, it's Josh. How are you?"

Josh was the older twin by five minutes and the one who was most like Jackson.

"Hi, son. I'm fine. How are you? How's your brother?" Jackson said pulling himself together.

"We're at Mom's till Wednesday. Would you like a visit?"

"Yes! I'm home for a few days. Sure, I'd like to get together," Jackson said as he walked to the kitchen for a beer. "Actually, what about you and Jared meeting me at Harry's this evening about six?"

"That sounds good. I'll ask Jared if he wants to go, but I'll be there for sure, Dad."

They talked a little longer, and then Josh said there were some things he needed to do.

Jackson was excited at the prospect of seeing his boys. He hasn't seen them since Christmas. The timing was perfect. He hoped Jared wouldn't show up. He loved Jared, but he was more like his mother in that he held grudges and was negative and judgmental at times. He always tried to push Jackson's buttons, and all that did was make Jackson angry, and Jackson was doing a good job keeping in control of his anger. The last thing he wanted to do was argue or defend himself.

He took a long shower, trimmed his beard, and got dressed. He wore his blue Levi's and a dark-blue Levi's T-shirt and his black and white Vans. He got his phone off the charger and saw two messages from Robert. *Oh shit.* He had forgotten that he was supposed to hang out with Robert that night. He texted him back saying that he was hanging out with his sons that night and that Robert was more than welcome to come.

Jackson got to Harry's at about 5:50 p.m. and got a table toward the back. He was a bit nervous about seeing his sons but also excited about it; he needed to see people who actually knew him—familiar faces. He was looking at his phone when he heard, "Dad!" He looked up, and there were his boys staring down at him. He got up and hugged them. They were a little taller than he was, and though they were identical, they looked different and always had; they had totally different styles.

Josh was more laid back; he was in jeans and a T-shirt, and his hair was short and a little messy. He had an easygoing personality. Jared on the other hand was more preppy; he took pride in how he dressed, which was in a polo shirt and cargo shorts with some Yeezys. His hair was also short, but he had dyed it blond, and he had an arrogant attitude.

"How you boys doing?" Jackson asked as he sat.

"We're good," Josh said looking at his brother.

They all ordered draft beers and started talking about nothing in particular. Jackson had just ordered another round of drinks when Robert walked up to them.

"Hey, Robert. Wasn't sure if you were gonna make it," Jackson said as he stood and shook Robert's hand. "Take a seat. Let me get you a beer." Jared looked at his brother and rolled his eyes. "Hey, boys, this here's my buddy Robert. These are my sons, Jared and Josh."

Everything went well for a while until they got a few drinks in them and Jared asked, "Dad, why did you think you needed to change jobs? Don't you think that was stupid and irresponsible?"

"He just wanted a change," Josh cut in before Jackson could reply.

"No, Josh, it's OK. I'll answer his question," Jackson said getting angry. "I did need a change. I wasn't happy, and I needed to do something different with my life. I thought I already told you that."

"When have you ever been happy, Dad?" Jared asked leaning in and staring at his father.

"Hey, listen," Josh said. "Can't we just sit here and have a good time?"

Jackson didn't say anything more. Jared had a good point. The truth was that he hadn't been content with where he was in life even before his divorce. "I'll be right back. Gotta take a leak," he said as he stood. He headed to the men's room to calm down; he was starting to get pissed.

Robert sat there feeling uncomfortable and awkward; he was just about to get up and make an excuse and leave when out of the blue Jared turned to him. "So, what about you?" he asked. "Robert, why are you here? How do you know my dad?"

"He's my friend, kind of my mentor when I started driving school. I'd just gotten out of the Marines and was looking for something else, and I guess we both clicked. We'll be working at the same company soon."

Jared just listened to this man, who was about his age, and felt jealous of him. He and his dad had never had a close relationship; his dad had always been there but had been distant at times, and they didn't have the same interests. Jared was angry at his dad and seeing this stranger in this close relationship with him pissed him off even more.

Jackson came out of the men's room after splashing water on his face to settle himself down and sober up. He didn't want to argue because when he did, he got loud and mean, and that was the last thing he wanted. But when he got back to the table, there was Jared and Robert already in an argument and he hadn't been away more than five minutes. "What's going on here?" Jackson yelled.

"Nothing, Dad," Jared said. "I was just listening to your buddy telling me what a great mentor and friend you are and that I should give you a break!"

Jackson looked and Robert. "I'm sorry about my son. Sometimes, he can be an ass."

"Don't apologize for me. You have no idea what's going on," Jared said getting up.

"Josh, what's going on?" Jackson asked, but Josh just sat there looking confused. "I don't know. I went to get another pitcher of beer, and here they were arguing."

"I really should get going," Robert said as he stood. "Sorry, Jackson. I'll see you around."

He left before Jackson could say anything. He felt bad and blindsided. "What the fuck was that all about?" Jackson yelled at Jared.

"I don't know. We got on the subject about him being in the Marines, and I was just asking him questions, but he didn't like that."

"Jared, you gotta be careful what you say to people and how you say it. You come across as judgmental at times," Jackson said.

That was true; Jared was always trying to tell people how to live their lives and giving his opinions when not even asked for them.

"You know what, Dad? You're just going through a midlife crisis and doing something stupid. You're gonna regret it. Watch!" Jared said getting up and heading for the door.

Jackson started to go after him, but Josh stopped him. "Just let it go, Dad. You know how he is. I never should have brought him. He has a problem with you changing careers. Sorry, Dad."

"It's OK, son. I just don't understand what his problem is with me." Jackson shook his head.

"He feels that you never really wanted a family, that you were faking it all these years, and becoming a trucker was your way of running away."

"I get it," Jackson said. "I was lost, and maybe I'm still not happy, but it has nothing to do with your mom or you boys. It's me. And I'm sorry I wasn't a better father."

"Dad, you don't have to apologize. You were a good-enough dad, and I don't think anyone is ever truly happy. Jared's the most unhappy person I know. He likes to blame others for that, and you're the lucky one who gets all the blame."

"I'll talk to him later one on one," Jackson said.

Jackson and Josh chitchatted for an hour about random things until Josh said, "I gotta get going, Dad."

They hugged each other and said their goodbyes. Jackson was sad to see Josh leave; he was probably the only person in Jackson's life who cared about him, and he felt lucky to have him.

The night was still young. Jackson texted Jared that he was sorry for whatever he had done or said that made him mad at him and that he loved him; he said that if he wanted to have a conversation, he'd listen.

He also texted Robert apologizing for whatever Jared had said. Jackson was feeling lonely, so he texted Emily, whom he hadn't seen in four months, and asked her if she wanted to come over. He was surprised when he got a text back right away from her saying it would be nice to get together.

He wasn't home longer than twenty minutes when he heard a knock on the door. There she was in just a pair of black leggings and a Johnny Cash T-shirt. Emily liked Jackson. He was in good shape for someone his age, and his eyes were intoxicating. She had been hurt when he didn't text or call her the whole time he was gone.

"Hey, girl! How you doing?" Jackson asked as he kissed her cheek and guided her into his apartment. He liked Emily. She was easy to be with and good in bed, but he didn't have feelings for her other than sex, and he hoped she felt the same way.

"I'm good," she said.

They talked for a little bit as they drank a few beers, and it wasn't long after that that they were in Jackson's bed having hot and heavy sex. Jackson wanted to make it last; he knew it would be a while before he'd have a night like this again.

The next morning, Jackson woke up late; Emily had left, and he was hungover and tired. It had been a full night. He looked at his phone and saw several messages from Jared, Robert, and Josh. Robert said that Jackson shouldn't feel bad about it, that it was OK, and that he should've not gone. He said he needed to stay away from bars and booze because he was on meds.

Jared on the other hand said, "It's all good, Dad. Sorry I was such an asshole," and Josh said that the next time they saw each other, it would be only the two of them. He texted them back and decided to stay home the next two days before he hit the road again.

Chapter 4

Two days later, Jackson woke up early; it was time to get back on the road. He was feeling good, rested, and though it hadn't been the best visit with his boys, he was happy to have seen them.

He got to the distribution center and saw his big, beautiful truck looking neglected and lonely. "I'm back!" he said as he got into the driver's seat. It was raining, and the freeways were full of commuters; traffic was heavy, and motorcyclists were weaving in and out of traffic. It seemed to him that every other car was an annoying Prius.

He figured it would be a long day. He sat back, turned on a podcast, and enjoyed the drive. His first stop was in Nevada, where he would pick up a trailer and take it to Tucson. He got to the truck stop he always went to just inside Nevada late in the afternoon. He ordered a burger and fries at the truck stop's restaurant.

"Long day?" the waitress asked when she came with his food.

"You can say that," Jackson said looking at her for the first time. He was so tired and preoccupied that he hadn't paid much attention to her when she had taken his order, but at that point, he was paying attention. Scarlet, according to her name tag, was pretty and petite and had nice breasts and shoulder-length brown hair and blue eyes. She wasn't a knockout or even young; she was at least in her late thirties, but he felt attracted to her.

"Anything else I can get you, just ask. I'm Scarlet." She was flirting with him. She came twice to refill his water. It was a slow afternoon, so she stayed and talked with him for a while. Jackson was so busy talking to her that he lost track of the time. *Oh shit!* he said, looking at his phone. "I gotta go. I gotta load to pick up in Vegas and get it back to Tucson by tomorrow morning." He felt bad about leaving; he really enjoyed talking to her.

"Here," she said when she came back with his bill and a note with her phone number. He gave her two twenties though his bill was only $12.

"Hey! You gave me too much," she said.

"Keep it," Jackson said. "Nice meeting you."

She watched him walk out hoping to see him again.

Jackson got to Tucson early the next day. He got to the truck stop after dropping off his load and wanted to get some sleep when he remembered the note Scarlet had given him and he had forgotten to read. He lay on his bed and read it: "Thank you for the conversation. I really enjoyed meeting you today. If you're ever in my neck of the woods again, I'd love to get together—Scarlet." He smiled as he fell asleep.

For the next three weeks, he drove through rain, fog, and even some snow; he was getting tired of this bipolar, miserable February weather. Jackson noticed that there weren't that many lot lizards at the truck stops. He thought that maybe it was the weather, but he learned that a serial killer was killing prostitutes; five had been found dead on Route 66. He felt bad for those women.

He was feeling lonely again and needed some female attention. He had a thirty-four-hour reset, so he decided to stay at the truck stop where Scarlet worked. He texted her: "Hello, Scarlet. I'm in your neck of the woods and would like to see you. I have thirty-four free hours!"

She replied in about thirty minutes: "Yes, I would love to get together! There's a bar just around the corner from the restaurant if you'd like to meet around six tonight."

It was noon, and he was tired. He got a room at a Motel 6 laid down and knocked out immediately. He woke up to his alarm on his phone going off. He showered and trimmed his beard. He put on his blue Levi's, a button-up plaid shirt, and his boots.

He got to the bar a little after six and saw her at the end of bar. Scarlet spotted him and stood. She looked pretty. She was wearing tight blue jeans with holes in the knees and a tight, long-sleeve black sweater. Her hair was down, and she had on very little makeup.

"Hello, Jackson," she said as he gave her a hug and sat next to her. They hit it off. Jackson was surprised about how he felt being with her;

he wasn't used to this feeling. He actually listened to her when she talked and found himself smiling and laughing more than usual.

It was late, and they were getting a little too tipsy. They found themselves very much into each other.

"Let's get out of here," Scarlet whispered.

"Where you wanna go?"

"To wherever you're staying," she said as she kissed him.

They walked to the motel laughing and flirting the whole way.

"Oh, shit. I forgot what room I'm in," Jackson said as he looked for the room key in his wallet. They laughed as Jackson fumbled around trying to open the door. They entered the room with only moonlight guiding their way. He started kissing her, and he lifted her up and sat her on the dresser. He finally got a hold of himself. "You sure you want to do this?"

"Yes, yes," she said as she pulled at his shirt.

They undressed each other and got into bed. They had sex at least three times that night.

Scarlet hadn't been with anyone for a while; she had gotten out of an abusive relationship just a year earlier and hadn't been with anyone since. She was starving for affection, and the minute she had seen Jackson, she knew she wanted him. She didn't care what his story was, or if he was married, or even if it would be just a one-night stand; all she wanted was to be held, to be looked at, and be desired even if it was just for one night.

The next day, Jackson woke up with Scarlet next to him. He wasn't sure how he felt about it. He didn't wake her; he slipped out of bed and showered. He put on his boxers and T-shirt, and when he opened the bathroom door, he saw that Scarlet was getting ready to leave. "Hey! Were you gonna sneak out on me?" Jackson said as he sat down next to her on the bed.

"Last night was great." Scarlet said as she got closer to him.

"Yes, it was," Jackson said and kissed her cheek. "I don't go back out on the road till late tonight. Are you off today?"

"Yeah, sure. Let me go home to shower and change. I'll come back with my car, and we can take the day from there."

"Sounds like a plan," he said.

But the minute she left, Jackson started having reservations: *Why did I invite her to spend the day with me?* He didn't ask women out on dates;

he just had hookups, and he wasn't looking for any sort of relationship. But for some reason, he wanted to spend more time with her.

Scarlet was back in an hour and looking good in jeans, a dark-grey hoodie, and hiking boots; her hair was in a tight ponytail. She also had sandwiches and snacks and water in her backpack. "I thought you might like to go to this hiking trail I often go to. It's a cool day, and no rain in sight."

"Sure. Why not?" he said. "Sounds like fun."

They hiked for a good two hours stopping here and there taking pictures of the scenery and some selfies and eating lunch on the trail. Jackson felt good to be out of the truck and enjoying the fresh, cool air.

When they got back to the motel, they were chitchatting about random stuff, nothing in particular, when Jackson decided he needed to talk to her about who he was and what he wanted; he felt that he owed it to her. "Listen, Scarlet. I had a really good time with you last night and today, and I don't want to mislead you about anyth—"

"Stop," Scarlet said. "It's OK. I get it. I know what you're gonna say, Jackson. It's fine."

"What was I going to say?"

"That you're not looking for anything serious, which is good 'cause neither am I."

"So, you're fine with this?"

"Yes, I am," she said as she started kissing him. "I like you. I like being with you even if it's temporarily. We don't need to talk about our feelings or our past or even what's going on with us now. Let's just enjoy each other and the time we have together no strings attached," she said kissing Jackson harder and deeper. She got up and straddled him on the bed.

Jackson didn't say anything as he flipped her on her back and got on top of her, and that was it … They were having sex. They both felt good; they both knew what the other one wanted as they make love in silence and then fell asleep exhausted.

Jackson woke up around 6:00 p.m., an hour before he needed to pick up his load. "Hey, wake up, Scarlet. I gotta get going."

He took a quick shower to wake himself up. When he got out, she was up and dressed. "OK then," Scarlet said, "I guess I'll see you when I see you."

"I'll text you when I'm back in town," Jackson said as he hurriedly packed his bag. He stopped and turned to Scarlet. "I had a good time!"

"Me too," she said.

They kissed, and she left.

It was cold night; the moon was full, and the stars were shining. He got in his truck and checked all the gauges and then got gas. It was a good night for a drive. He felt good and rested, and he still had the images of himself and Scarlet together and was missing her a little. He was on his way back to California to drop off the trailer in Modesto before he picked up another in Stockton.

Just as he was driving back into California, he saw many highway patrol cruisers on the side of the highway. The traffic was slow. Jackson didn't think it had been an accident. When he got closer, he saw a body covered by a blanket. Jackson knew it must have been something very bad. He found out later that night that it was the body of a prostitute, the sixth they had found in six months.

He got back to the distribution center and was ready for a break; he wanted to get back to his apartment and sleep in his own bed, but he was thinking about Scarlet; he wanted to call or text her, but he wasn't sure that was a good idea.

He went into the office to get some more logbooks and a couple of work shirts that had been waiting there for him for months when Keith came toward him. "Oh my God, man! You look good!" Jackson said as he shook Keith's his hand.

"Thanks buddy!" Keith said. "I owe it all to you and Robert."

"You wanna get a drink?" Jackson asked. "That's if you have time."

"Why not? I don't hit the road till Friday."

They went for drinks; Jackson felt good hanging out with Keith and talking shop. Then they got on the subject of the murders.

"Can you fuckin' believe what's going on?" Keith asked. "They think it's a truck driver killing those women."

Jackson listened to Keith and got the scoop on the murders; he told Keith what he had seen on the highway on his way back to California.

"Well, I really ought to get going," Keith said as he looked at his phone.

"See you around," Jackson said. "By the way, have you seen Robert lately?"

"Yes, last week. He seemed kind of out of it, stressed out or something. I tried talking to him, but he blew me off."

"I'll call him tomorrow," Jackson said.

Jackson got back to his apartment feeling lonely. He thought about texting Emily, but he couldn't stop thinking about Scarlet.

The next day, Jackson called Robert to see if he wanted to come over for a visit, but he was out on the road. "Hey, listen. I just wanted to ask how you're doing," Jackson said.

"I'm good," Robert replied keeping the conversation short.

Jackson hung up feeling concerned about Robert and hoping he was doing well mentally and physically. Jackson was actually excited to hit the road again doing the same routes—Nevada to Arizona and then back to Vegas. He texted Scarlet asking if she was free to hook up. He was excited about seeing her again. He still didn't understand his feelings for her, but he certainly had some.

Chapter 5

Jackson pulled into the truck stop late; he thought that Scarlet would be sleeping, but when he turned off his truck and looked at his phone, he saw that she had texted him: "Whatever time you get here, text me. I'll pick you up. You can stay with me till you go back out on the road."

He immediately texted her back, and before he had his backpack together, there Scarlet was in her blue Nissan Sentra waiting for him. They got to her one-bedroom house after picking up some takeout.

Jackson walked into her house and saw that it was put together nicely for such a small space—a couch and recliner in the living room and a small table in the kitchen. He saw some beautiful framed black and white photos on the walls. The house was laid back and simple, which made the place look and feel bigger.

They ate the takeout and drank some red wine. It was a nice, cool night. They couldn't take their eyes off each another, but the conversation was short because neither wanted to ask any personal questions or talk about themselves; they didn't want to ruin the night.

Finally, after about a good hour of eating and small talk, Scarlet cleaned up the kitchen while Jackson took a shower; he felt dirty from his long day of driving. He used her pink strawberry shampoo and her coconut body wash. Her bathroom was decorated grey and white with little hints of red. He got into boxers and a white T-shirt. He was tired and sore from driving all day.

Scarlet was in her bedroom trying to get all sexy in her all-black nightie with her hair down. She had been anticipating this night for weeks. She was totally sprung on Jackson. She had thought that she wasn't into sex anymore, but after spending time with Jackson, she realized what she'd been missing. She hated having wasted her thirties with an abusive, selfish man.

"You look absolutely beautiful!" Jackson said when he saw her lying on the bed looking sexy as hell. He took off his shirt and looked at her. He wanted it to be special for her; she'd been nothing but generous to him. He started out slowly. He kissed her from head to toe as she moaned and closed her eyes taking in every touch, every kiss. Never in all her forty years of life had a man ever made her feel that good … By the end of the night, she had had two orgasms. They fell asleep in each other's arms feeling fulfilled and satisfied.

The next morning, they woke up at the same time and made love again; they couldn't get enough of each other. They showered together not really saying much, and Scarlet distracted herself by making breakfast.

"Smells good," Jackson said as he sat at the kitchen table. "It's been a long time since I've eaten breakfast."

"It's been a long time since I've made breakfast," she said, and they laughed.

Jackson couldn't believe he was letting this happen to him. He felt nervous. He didn't want Scarlet to see the mean, selfish asshole he could be, but he could also be different, he told himself; he didn't have to be that person anymore. He'd been good the last few months. He decided to just go with the flow and not have any expectations, to enjoy his time with her while it lasted.

The rest of the day, they hung out at her house. He did some yard work and made some repairs around the house, and she shopped for dinner.

Scarlet couldn't help but have feelings for Jackson. She didn't want those feelings, but they came to her anyway.

"Thanks for cleaning up my yard," she said as they sat down for an early dinner.

"It's the least I could do. You've been so good to me," he said as he poured wine for them.

After dinner, Jackson cleared the plates while Scarlet started doing the dishes. They sat on the couch to watch a movie, and Scarlet snuggled up close to Jackson; she felt good being in his strong arms. They fell asleep on the couch.

Early the next morning, Scarlet woke up to Jackson's carrying her to the bed. "I got to get going soon," Jackson said as he lay her down and started kissing her; they make love once again before he left.

Scarlet drove him back to his truck a little early. She needed to be at work at noon. Their special time was over. Jackson gave her $200 saying that he wanted to help her out that way; he said he was making good money driving and didn't have anything to spend it on. Scarlet tried to resist it, but Jackson insisted.

"Drive safely," she said as she watched him get in his truck. There was so much Scarlet wanted to talk to him about, so much she wanted to ask him, so much she wanted to share with him about herself. They had promised to keep it casual, but being with him made her realize that she actually wanted a relationship, a partner, someone to spend her life with.

Jackson did nothing but drive the next few weeks straight; it was a busy time for the company. He had seen Scarlet a few more times. Though those visits were brief, every time was special, and he left with more feelings for her. He couldn't wait to see her again.

He ran across Robert at a truck stop outside Stockton. He couldn't believe his eyes at first; he didn't recognize him. He looked different, thinner. His hair was longer, and he looked unkempt, which surprised Jackson because Robert had always looked put together.

"Hey Robert!" Jackson yelled waving.

Robert turned around and saw Jackson. He wasn't sure how he felt about it.

"Long time no see," Jackson said as they shook hands. "How you been? How's work?"

"Real good," Robert said.

"I've texted you," Jackson said.

"Yeah, I got them. Sorry I didn't reply. I've just been trying to get used my new life. You know how it is."

"Sure, sure, I get it. Have you been going to your meetings and taking your meds?" Jackson knew how important those meetings were for Robert, who was battling PTSD and past addictions.

"Yeah, sure," Robert said looking away and feeling guilty because he hadn't gone to a single meeting since he'd started driving. "Listen, Jackson," Robert said looking at his phone. "I gotta get going."

Jackson knew by the way Robert was acting that something was wrong. "Hey, Robert, if you ever need to talk, call me. I'm a good listener, man. I'm sorry for not having really been there for you the last couple of times we were together."

"Yeah, sure," Robert said, "but really, I'm OK."

But the truth was that he wasn't.

Jackson was happy when he finally got dispatched to his regular routes again. He really needed to see Scarlet; he was feeling lonely. And he had other stuff on his mind. He couldn't shake off how his encounter with Robert had gone, and he kept thinking about the prostitutes' murders.

He hit the road early the next day hoping to make good time, but there was lots of traffic on his way to Vegas from Tucson. A huge pileup kept him in traffic for hours. He wasn't going to get to the truck stop and meet up with Scarlet because his driving hours were running out. He couldn't believe his bad luck.

After about several hours on the highway, he got to a truck stop outside Vegas, about forty-five miles from the one he usually stopped at. He got a room in a motel around the corner and texted Scarlet to see if she wanted to meet him there; he told her about not having enough driving hours left.

She immediately texted back saying yes. She needed to see Jackson; she knew she wasn't supposed to, but she needed to talk to him. She was falling in love with him, and she wanted to tell him that. She also needed to tell him about her son in Phoenix. She was realizing that she wanted a relationship, a partner, and being with Jackson made her realize that she needed not to be scared anymore, that she needed to open herself up again after her horrible relationship with her ex-boyfriend Chad. She had also gone out on a date with someone who had been wanting to go out with her for a while, and she wanted to tell all this to Jackson. She knew that it might be the last time she'd ever see him.

Jackson had to wait a while for Scarlet; she would come right after she got off work. He was bored. He had about twenty-four free hours before he was supposed to hit the road again. He started drinking. He hadn't drunk that much since he'd been driving, but for some reason, he felt like drinking. He had so many things on his mind, and he had these strong feelings for Scarlet, which he was trying hard to deny.

She got to the motel late nervous and excited at the same time. She was also scared to be out that late at night with that serial killer out there. She knew of a waitress in Vegas who had been killed. She wanted to tell Jackson about her past, a past she was not proud of. It had taken her a while before she could actually be happy with herself again and feel worthy.

Jackson heard a knock on the door. He had dozed off; he was tired after the long day of driving and from the drinking; he was halfway through a pint of vodka. Jackson got up stumbling and went to the door.

Chapter 6

"About time you got here," Jackson said as he opened the door.

Scarlet realized that he had been drinking not just by the half-empty bottle of vodka on the end table but also by his demeanor. She was totally put off and sad; it reminded her right away of Chad, and she didn't like it.

"Well, you gonna give me a kiss or what?" Jackson asked slurring his words a little.

She hugged and kissed him, and he squeezed her hard and gave her a sloppy kiss; she tasted vodka on his lips.

"So how was the drive up here?" he asked as he let her go and fell onto the bed; he was feeling off balance.

"It was good," she said still standing there.

"Hey, get comfortable. Relax. Have a drink. It's late. You must be tired," Jackson said as he poured some vodka for himself.

Scarlet looked around and felt uncomfortable; she wanted to get back in her car and take off. At least that was what her head was telling her, but her heart wanted to be with him more than anything. She sat on the chair across from Jackson. "I came here to talk to you, Jackson. I know we said we were gonna keep this casual, but I've developed feelings for you that I can't deny anymore."

Jackson sat up and looked at her. He was drunk and horny. "Hey, I didn't invite you here to have a fuckin' conversation!" He couldn't help himself; when he felt some sort of way and had been drinking, he would say anything that came to his head. That was why he had had problems in all his relationships.

"Jackson, it's not all about what you want. I didn't come all this way to just have sex with you. I wanted to have an adult conversation."

Jackson looked at her. "OK, go ahead." He didn't have the energy to argue.

"I want more, Jackson! Being with you made me feel that I want to be in a relationship again. My last relationship was bad, really bad!" Scarlet said getting emotional. "I know you said you weren't looking for anything serious, but I am now. I also wanted to tell you that I've started seeing someone else."

Jackson took in all she said. He wasn't sure how to react. He didn't want to be an asshole, but her seeing someone else pissed him off. "What the fuck?" he said getting off the bed. "I thought you weren't a whore! I guess I was wrong." He fell back on the bed.

Scarlet couldn't believe it. This man she had fallen hard for turned out to be just like every other man. *How could I have been so fuckin' stupid?* She started getting her stuff together as tears filled her eyes. "You're unbelievable. I can't believe you just said that to me. I thought we had something special. I thought you were special! But you're not. You're just another asshole! And all I did was waste my time!"

She headed for the door and tried to unlock it. Jackson just looked at her as she struggled to open the door. He didn't want to let her go, not like this. *Why am I such an asshole? I didn't mean what I said.* "Stop!" He went over to her. "I'm sorry." He turned her around and hugged her. "I'm just drunk and maybe a little jealous." He guided her to the bed.

She sat next to him and saw the sadness in his eyes as he repeatedly apologized. He put his arm around her. "If you wanna talk, I'll listen." He was buzzing, and he felt bad. He wasn't thinking about how this would all play out; he was just thinking about the present.

Scarlet looked at Jackson and couldn't help herself. She had been craving intimacy when they first met, but she had also been craving friendship, someone to talk to. There was so much that she had kept inside for so long that she had never shared with anyone.

Scarlet lay her head on Jackson's chest, and they lay back on the bed. "I have a son in Phoenix," she said. "He's fifteen. He lives with his father. We never got married; we just shared custody until I got in a relationship with someone who wasn't good for me or my son. We were doing drugs and drinking, and he was very abusive toward me, so I gave full custody of my son to his dad."

She started crying. "I was weak and broken. This man Chad had total control of me until I finally had had enough and tried to leave him. I came here to Nevada to get away from him, but he found me and almost killed me," she said in between sobs as Jackson held her and stroked her back. Images of that day came to her mind. "He's in prison now for attempted murder, and I've been sober ever since."

Jackson listened to her. He couldn't believe it. She had seemed so strong and independent, but her past seemed like a sad Lifetime movie. He felt sorry for her but also overwhelmed by her story. She needed a better, stronger, more-giving man than him. He hugged her and kissed away her tears not saying a word. He just held her until she started kissing him back. They sat up and took off each other's clothes. Their lovemaking was long and passionate; she held onto Jackson not wanting the moment to end.

Jackson let himself go for that one night. He told her things he had never thought he would tell a woman. They talked into the night.

"I just wanted you to know all this, Jackson, because I love you. I understand if it's too much for you, but I'm hoping it's not, and you don't have to be jealous, Jackson, I only have eyes for you."

Those were the last words Scarlet said before they drifted off to sleep.

Jackson woke up first the next morning feeling like crap. He ran to the bathroom throwing up anything and everything; he was really regretting the vodka he had drunk the previous night. As he showered, he thought about everything they had said the previous night, and he couldn't believe that he had allowed it to get that serious.

"Jackson!" Scarlet said knocking on the bathroom door. "Can I get in there really quick? I need to go. I work at noon today."

He opened the door reluctantly; there she was looking at him. "Hey," she said as she kissed him. "Sorry if I was a bit dramatic last night, and thank you, honey, for listening to me. It really means a lot."

She came out of the bathroom feeling that a weight had been lifted off her chest. She was sitting on the bed putting on her shoes when Jackson came back with two coffees. "Oh my God thank you! I so need this," Scarlet said taking the coffee. "Hey! You heard about those murders?"

"I certainly have," Jackson said. "It's all over the news."

"I'm scared," Scarlet said. "A waitress in Vegas was found murdered a couple of weeks ago."

"Was she a prostitute too?" Jackson asked.

"No, she wasn't," Scarlet said feeling a little angry that Jackson would have asked that.

"I'm sorry I asked," Jackson said, "but most of the victims were."

"She was a waitress like me at one of the casinos at the state line. I'm scared, Jackson," Scarlet said again hoping for a little compassion.

Jackson just looked at her; he really didn't feel that she was in any danger, so it was hard for him to feel any sympathy, and he didn't know what she wanted him say. The fact was that he was hungover and sick and tired. He was supposed to be back on the road by six that night, and he needed rest.

She could tell he wasn't feeling well. She went up to him. "I love you. I'm gonna say it 'cause it's how I feel, and I want more than anything to be with you. Tell me now, Jackson, if you want to call it off. Let me know so I can go on with my life."

He couldn't say anything at that point. He just desperately wanted to sleep. To make it easy for himself, he said, "I'll see you in a week or so."

"OK," Scarlet said, "because I was thinking of visiting my son in Phoenix next week to get out of town for a while away from the psychopath who's roaming the highway, but if you're gonna visit in a week or so, I'll wait till next month."

Jackson hugged her. When he let her go, he felt sad thinking that it might be the last time he would see her. Everything she had told him the previous night scared him; she had way too much baggage, and the last thing he needed was to worry about someone other than himself. He was way too selfish for that.

On her drive home, Scarlet kept kicking herself thinking she shouldn't have told him everything. She had been feeling vulnerable and needed someone to talk to. She was scared that she'd never see him again.

Jackson slept hard for the next few hours but woke up still feeling physically and emotionally drained. He really wished that she hadn't confided all that to him. He felt different about the whole relationship.

He was ready to get back out on the road, get home, and leave this whole mess behind him. He cared about Scarlet but way more than he wanted to. He couldn't allow it to go any further; it was getting too complicated.

Chapter 7

Jackson got a couple of loads done in California over the next few weeks before making his way back to Modesto. He'd given the routes that would have taken him through Nevada to another driver. He wasn't ready to see Scarlet again.

The days seemed long and lonely; he tried to drown his thoughts by listening to podcasts or music, but that didn't work. All he could think about was Scarlet, who had even entered his dreams. He remembered the desperation on her face when she told him about her past. He still felt her in his arms. *Get yourself together*, he told himself as he got to Modesto. He was ready for a few days off and sleeping in his own bed, going to his regular hangouts, and maybe even hooking up with Emily so she could help him get Scarlet off his mind.

At the distribution center, he backed up his truck like a pro. He collected his laundry, cleaned up his sleeper, and was off. He got home late; he paid the Uber driver and immediately went to sleep.

The next morning, he woke up feeling restless. He wasn't sure what to do with his free time. He did his laundry including his blankets and sheets. He made some breakfast, worked out, finished up his laundry, and showered.

He washed his dirty pickup and got its oil changed. He got himself a much-needed haircut. He shopped for groceries and called Josh with an invite to dinner. He needed a distraction, to be around someone he could actually talk to, someone who didn't ask anything of him. He got his house in order. He wanted Josh to be proud of him, to think he was doing well. But to be honest, he wasn't. He had this ache in his chest; he missed Scarlet more than he ever thought he could.

Josh showed up right on time; he was happy to have one-on-one time with his dad. He hadn't seen him since the whole shit show at Harry's.

"Hey, son, how're you doing?" Jackson said as he opened the door.

"Good, Dad. How are you? You look tired." He gave his dad a quick hug.

"I'm good, just a little tired."

They went to the kitchen, where Jackson pulled two Heinekens from the fridge. He hadn't drunk since that last night with Scarlet.

"Smells good, Dad. What're you cooking?"

"Steak, mashed potatoes, and asparagus."

It had been a long time since Jackson had cooked. He thought about making for Scarlet what he had made for Josh, but it was too late; too much time had gone by. He thought that whatever they had had was over.

As they ate, they talked about Jared's getting a job in LA doing graphic design, which he had gone to school for. "That's awesome," Jackson said. "I'm happy he's doing well. And what about you, Josh?"

"I'm working at a youth center for at-risk kids. I'm going back to school for my master's so I can be a social worker."

"I'm so proud of both my sons."

They talked and drank, and Jackson started just talking about everything; that's what happened when he drank. "So, you got a lady, Josh?"

"Yes, Dad, I thought I told you about Missy. I met her at school. She's so cool! We have so much in common. I'll bring her next time we get together. And you, Dad? You got a woman?"

"No, not really."

"Why not? You've been divorced for over a year, and Mom's moved on. You deserve to be happy too, Dad."

"I was kinda seeing someone ..." Jackson couldn't help himself; it just came out. He hadn't planned on talking about Scarlet, but he felt he had to. "It was supposed to be just something casual, not serious. We met up a few times, and things started getting serious. It was so intense the last time I saw her."

"Do you care about her, Dad?"

"Yes, I guess so, but it's too much, Josh. She told me some personal stuff about herself, and she even said she loved me. I can't deal with that!

I'm not looking for anything serious. I don't think I'm going to see her anymore," Jackson said putting his head down and feeling guilty.

"Are you fuckin' serious, Dad? This woman opened up to you, said she loved you, and you're going to do her like that? That's typical you, Dad! Unbelievable!" Josh shook his head in disgust.

"So, what do you think I should do?" Jackson asked feeling blindsided by Josh's reaction.

"Don't know, Dad. Maybe not be such a selfish asshole, but I guess that's just who you are."

"What the fuck does that mean?" Jackson said standing up and feeling defensive. He had never expected to hear something like that from Josh of all people.

"Dad, this is exactly why you have such a fucked-up relationship with Jared and anyone else who enters your life. It's like if anything gets too complicated or serious, you bail. You've done that ever since I can remember!" Josh said standing and going for his jacket.

"So what? You gonna shit on me and just take off?"

"I'm not shitting on you, Dad. I'm just letting you know that that's what you do. If you care about this woman and she makes you feel good and she actually loves you, you owe it to yourself and to her to see if you can develop something. If you keep pushing people away, you're gonna find yourself a lonely old man."

That made sense to Jackson. "OK, sit down, Josh. You're right. I do that … I push people away."

Josh felt sorry for his dad, who looked so defeated. He hadn't wanted to yell at him or make him feel bad, but he felt he had to for his dad's sake. He loved him and wanted the best for him.

Jackson and Josh talked more into the night, and Josh left feeling good because Jackson had agreed to give Scarlet a call. And Jackson went to bed feeling a whole different way; Josh had made him think about things.

The next morning, Jackson cleaned up from the previous night and thought about the conversation he and Josh had had. He was scheduled to get back on the road late that afternoon and pick up a load in Vegas. He decided to see Scarlet again. He had to. He wasn't sure what he would say to her or if they would even be together any longer, but he owed it to her and himself to at least give it a chance. He realized he really didn't want to be alone.

Chapter 8

Jackson was getting his stuff together for the long drive. He was looking forward to it; he was going to make a point to see Scarlet. He was on the couch and eating a sandwich when he heard on the news some more about the murders. Another body had been found—a forty-year-old Nevada resident. Her name was Scarlet Malone, a waitress at a truck stop.

Jackson couldn't believe what he was hearing. *Is this true? Was she really killed?* He felt sick. He ran to the bathroom and threw up. He sat on the bathroom floor feeling devastated and guilty—very guilty. He felt responsible.

Scarlet had opened up to him that night telling him about her feelings, her past, and her fears of this serial killer. Jackson hadn't been able to give her the compassion she needed; all he had thought about was himself; he was sure she had been overreacting. He should have really listened to her, should have told her to go to Phoenix to get out of town for a while. *Why am I such an asshole?*

Jackson knew it was his fault. He knew he could have done so much more for her. She had been in love with him, and he had been realizing that he really cared for her too. *Why didn't I just open up to her, listen more intently, when she told me about her fears and give her some advice on how to protect herself? That's all she was looking for—someone to care about her.*

He thought of how devastated and used and hurt she must have felt when he hadn't called her in a month. He pulled himself together. He knew at that moment that he had to do something. He owed it to Scarlet. He was determined to do everything in his power to find this killer, to find the person who had taken the life of a promising young woman and many others. He finally admitted to himself that he had been falling for her too. He wished he had told her that.

He couldn't just go back to work. He had business to take care of in Nevada. He had the money and had racked up enough paid time off to take a short break. He got his stuff together as if he were a robot. He was going to make things happen. He wouldn't sit back and forget about Scarlet as if she had been irrelevant. She mattered, and he cared about her. He regretted that it had taken such an unimaginable act of pure evil for him to realize it.

He booked a room for a week at the motel by the truck stop; he wanted to be close to where she was when she had been killed. He wasn't a private detective or a cop, but he was a truck driver who knew truck drivers, and he would do whatever he could to help find this killer. *This has been going on way too long. Why haven't the cops found the killer yet? Was it not a priority because the victims were mainly hookers?* Jackson too had been guilty of thinking less of these murders because they were prostitutes, but they were people like everyone else; they deserved to be remembered, and they deserved justice.

Jackson called up Josh, the only one he had told about Scarlet. Josh couldn't believe what his dad was telling him at first; he thought he was lying because they had been talking about her just the night before. He felt so bad for his dad; he heard guilt and depression in his voice, but he was really surprised at his dad's determination to help find the killer. He thought his dad was being a bit delusional thinking that he could help, but he also knew that his dad was serious and that he felt extremely guilty and that he had to do it. All Josh could do over the phone was console him and encourage him.

Jackson hit the road early in the afternoon of a cold, overcast, gloomy day just like he felt. He had told his boss that he needed some time off for a family emergency. The sun was setting when he crossed into Nevada. Thoughts of Scarlet came to him. How broken she had been that night, she had cried on his chest and spilled her heart out. How he hadn't given her what she had needed that night. *Would I have been a better listener if I'd been sober?* He didn't know; he just had to put it behind him. He couldn't go back; he had to move forward and do all he could to find justice for her and the other victims.

He got to the motel late. He went to the restaurant she had worked at and remembered the first time he had seen her and how kind she had been, how she had flirted with him.

"Hello. What can I get you?" a waitress asked as he sat at table in the middle of the restaurant, which wasn't crowded considering the late hour.

"I'll have a cheeseburger, fries, and a Diet Coke," he said making sure to look at the waitress that time.

When she came back with his Diet Coke, he said after looking at her name tag, "Christine, can I ask you a couple of questions?"

"Yes, sure," she said. She was obviously attracted to him.

"It's about Scarlet."

Christine's heart sank when she heard her name. Then she looked at him a little closer and remembered Scarlet telling her about this good-looking trucker she was seeing. "Oh my God! Are you Jackson?"

"Yes I am," Jackson said looking a bit confused.

"Scarlet told me all about you. Let me get your food. I'll clock out and talk to you while you eat, OK?"

"Yes, please."

They talked for a good thirty minutes; Christine talked a mile a minute about Scarlet and how she had been so into him, how she had been waiting for him to come back to town, how devastated she had been when he hadn't called her.

"Listen," Jackson said cutting her off. "I know I was an asshole. I really should have called her and not left her hanging, but I did. So now I feel like shit, believe me. I was really gonna come and see her and talk to her, but it's too late, and I'm a hundred percent guilty of that, but I'm here now trying to make up for it, so please, can you tell me about that night and anything you remember?"

Christine realized why Scarlet had been so into Jackson. His eyes were mesmerizing, and she felt a little flush in his presence. "I told the cops everything I remembered."

"Well now tell me everything too," Jackson said.

"OK. It was normal night, nothing out of the ordinary. Scarlet was off at 2:00 a.m., and she was parked close by, so she didn't ask anyone to walk her out. But when the manager left at 4:00 a.m., he saw Scarlet's car still out there."

"Did she have any unusual customers? Any who looked shady or out of place?"

"No, not really. I had left just before she did, so I didn't see her leave, just what Marvin told me."

"Who's Marvin?"

"He's the cook and night manager. He's working right now. That's all I can tell you."

"OK, that's good. I'll talk to Marvin next. I'm going by the police station tomorrow."

He waited for Marvin to get off work, which he did in an hour. Jackson saw a large, bald guy with a dirty white apron coming toward him.

"I hear you wanted to talk to me," Marvin said going up to Jackson.

"Yes. I heard you were the last person to see or hear from Scarlet the night she died."

The two shook hands. "Hey, guy, no disrespect, but who are you?" Marvin asked.

"I'm Jackson Thomas, a good friend of Scarlet's, and I'm here just trying to help out, OK, guy?" Jackson asked feeling annoyed.

"Listen, Jackson," Marvin said, "I said everything I knew to the cops, OK? And you're not law enforcement or even family. So I'm not going to answer any of your questions."

Marvin got up and started walking away, but Jackson stood and got in his way. "I don't know what your deal is, but I don't see how it would hurt for you to give me a little information. Don't you care about your employees?" Jackson said raising his voice. This guy was pissing Jackson off with his nonchalant, I don't give a fuck attitude.

Marvin stepped back feeling intimidated by Jackson. "All I can say is that she left work at two. No one walked her out. It was just the two of us, and she said she'd be fine, and that was that. Then when I got off at four, I saw that her car was still there. That's all I know, OK? Now are we finished?"

"Yes, we're finished." Jackson felt that this whole visit had been a waste of time.

Chapter 9

Jackson woke up the next morning feeling restless. He was determined to get some answers and help the cops in any way he could. He knew that they thought the killer was a truck driver, so he was hoping they would like to hear from him.

At the local police station, he talked to a few cops, who looked at him as if he were crazy. They told him to call the two detectives who were working on the case. Considering Jackson had known the last victim, he thought they would talk to him.

He met them later that afternoon; they had driven from Barstow.

"Hello. I'm Detective Anthony Brown, and this is my partner, Detective Melissa Ruiz," Brown said shaking Jackson's hand.

Brown was a black man in his late forties who has been a detective for about eight years. He was tall—at least six-two—and Jackson could tell that he worked out and cared about his appearance by the way he carried himself. He was dressed sharp in dress pants, shirt, and tie.

Ruiz was in her midthirties and very petite with dark-brown hair in a tight bun. She was wearing grey dress pants and a white long-sleeve blouse. Jackson thought she was pretty.

"So we were told you had information about the Route 66 serial killer," Ruiz said as she too shook his hand. She had been a detective for barely a year; she had worked her ass off for her promotion from patrol officer, which she had been since right out of college. She knew she needed to prove herself to get her peers' respect. This case was very hard on her, but she was hoping to find the killer soon.

"No, not exactly information, Detective," Jackson answered, "but I did know Scarlet Malone. She was a friend of mine, a lover actually,"

Jackson said knowing they would ask him about that sooner or later. "We saw each other a few times. The last time was about four weeks ago. She told me about her fear of this serial killer. I thought she was overreacting. I thought that only prostitutes were targeted."

"So do you know anything that can help the case?" Brown asked.

"All I know is that y'all think it's a truck driver and I'm a truck driver, so if you have any questions about truck driving or drivers, I'm here to answer them."

The detectives asked him a few questions, and Ruiz said, "So exactly what do you think you can do? And why are you here? You didn't know this woman that long, and it seems that you cut her loose four weeks ago. Isn't that right?"

"Detective, if you're saying that to make me feel guilty, you don't have to. I feel guilty enough. That's why I'm here, and that's why I'm staying. I don't think that you police have been doing your job! This killer has been out there for months, and you mean to tell me that you don't have any leads? That's bad! Maybe y'all don't give a shit 'cause you think these women don't matter, but they do. I'm here to find some justice for them! And by the way, this women has a name—Scarlet."

Jackson had had enough. He left. *Maybe I'm being delusional. Why am I here? What am I gonna do?* He couldn't answer that, but it was as if something was leading him.

"Hey wait up," Ruiz yelled as she ran after Jackson. "Sorry if I was pushing you. I know you're just trying to help, so here." She handed him her card. "If you have questions or information no matter how small, call us, let us know. We're doing everything in our power to find this killer."

Jackson looked at her card. "We all need to do better."

Jackson drove back to the motel. He was exhausted, and he fell asleep immediately. The next morning, he was feeling defeated. He had wanted to make a different life for himself by becoming a truck driver, but his new life was turning into shit, he thought. He hadn't recognized something that was good for him until it was too late.

He went to the restaurant for breakfast. Memories of Scarlet came to him, how he had been immediately attracted to her the day they met.

"Hello. So I see you're back," Christine said.

"Still here," Jackson said.

"Listen, Jackson," she said guiding him to a table. "I'm sorry about last time I saw you, but I do have some information I didn't tell the cops," she said sitting close to him so no one could hear.

"What is it?"

"I saw Scarlet talking to a guy earlier that day. He was average height, slim and young. There was something about his eyes. The way he was looking at her was creepy. I totally forgot about that till this morning."

"Do you know if he was a truck driver?"

"I don't know if he was or wasn't. And also, Jackson, I'm sorry about what happened. I can tell you really cared for her."

He just nodded at that. She took his order, and they didn't talk anymore about it. Christine sensed that Jackson was deep in thought and wanted to be left alone.

That night, Jackson went to three truck stops just checking things out and looking for anyone suspicious or shady. There weren't many lot lizards out because of the murders. He kept thinking about what Christine had said about the young man Scarlet had talked with. There weren't really many young truck drivers. The youngest one he knew was Robert. *But no way it could be him.* Jackson tried to get the thought out of his head but couldn't.

The next morning, he woke up with a whole other approach. He was going to try to work with the detectives; he believed Ruiz really cared. He called her.

"Hello, Detective Ruiz. This is Jackson Thomas. I'm calling to see if you wanted to get together so we could talk about the case. I may have some information for you."

"I'll be back in Nevada today. I can come over to your motel room, or we can meet somewhere else," she said realizing how inappropriate she had sounded. They agreed to meet at his motel room.

By the time Ruiz got there, the maid had cleaned the room. The curtains were open. She didn't understand why she felt nervous, but she did.

Jackson opened the door and thought that the detective looked different. Her hair was down, and she was wearing glasses. "Hello, and come in."

"So what information do you have for me?" Ruiz asked as they sat at the table. She opened her note pad.

"I talked to Christine, a waitress at the restaurant where Scarlet worked, and she told me about a young guy she had seen Scarlet talking to earlier that day. He was young, thin, and of average height, but she said there was something about his eyes. The way he had looked at Scarlet made Christine feel uneasy."

Ruiz wrote down everything and then looked at him expecting more details. "Is that it?"

"Yes, pretty much," Jackson said. He stood and went to the window. "What do you have? Any suspects you're looking at?"

"I can't tell you that or anything about the case."

"Then why are you here?" Jackson felt himself getting pissed.

"I'm here," Ruiz said standing and getting her notes together, "because you told me you had information I could use, but that's not what I'm seeing."

"Listen, Detective Ruiz, let's work together. Any information is better than none at all!"

Chapter 10

Jackson watched Ruiz leave. She hadn't told him that they would work together, but she had said that she would keep him updated.

He kept thinking about Robert. He decided to call him to see how he was doing and find out if he had been at the truck stops where the women had been murdered, but he didn't think it was the time to tell Ruiz about his suspicions. He didn't have the authority to call his job and get Robert's routes, but he knew that if he saw or sensed anything at all in his conversation with Robert, he'd let the detectives know.

"Hello, Robert. How're you doing?"

"I … I'm fine," Robert stuttered. He sounded nervous to Jackson. "How are you? I heard you took a leave of absence for a family emergency." Robert thought that that was a little suspicious.

Jackson ignored his question. "So how's work? How are you? Have you been going to your meetings? You seemed a little stressed the last time I saw and talked to you, and I know how important those meetings are for you."

"Yeah, sure, everything's fine!" Robert said not wanting a lecture. "You know what, Jackson? Don't worry about me or what I'm doing or not doing. Just take care of your family emergency. I gotta go!" He hung up.

Jackson kicked himself. He shouldn't have gone at Robert like that. He should've eased his way in before giving him any lecture. He didn't know what to do, so he ended up calling Keith.

"Hey, what's up, my brother?" Keith said.

"Nothing much, guy," Jackson said.

"Are you OK? I heard you were on a leave of absence."

"I'm good, but I wanted to ask you about Robert. I don't think he's doing too well, and I'm worried about him."

"Yeah, he, *ummm*, got in a little trouble a few weeks ago, Jackson."

"What was it?"

"He was going to Vegas to pick up a load and was out of communication for, like, two days. No one knew where he was. I had to pick up the load."

"Where had he been? What was he up to?" Jackson said feeling himself getting a little excited; he wanted to calm down before Keith got suspicious.

They talked for at least thirty minutes. Keith told him where he had had to pick up the load and drop it off. He also told Jackson about the truck stop in the area. Jackson was writing down everything. Jackson also found out that when he had changed his routes, Robert was the one who had taken them over. He felt he would puke. He was sweating. He had to take some deep breaths and get himself together. He realized that if he hadn't changed his routes, Robert would never have been in the area.

"What's this all about?" Keith asked getting a bit suspicious.

"I was just wondering about Robert. Did they ever find out what was up with Robert those two days?"

"He told Jim that he'd had a bit of a nervous breakdown."

"And Jim let him drive?"

"Yeah. Why not? It wasn't a big deal, man. We all go through some shit. And he's a veteran, man. Why you getting on him?"

Jackson knew that Keith was getting upset and that he owed it to Keith to let him know something. "Keith, I can't tell you everything right now, but there's some bad shit going on, and I'm in the middle of it, and I think Robert may be too."

"What is it? Talk to me!"

"I can't. Not now, but soon. Just do me a favor—don't tell Robert about our conversation. I gotta go. I'm expecting an important phone call." He hung up before Keith could reply.

But then his phone did ring. "Hello, Jackson. This is Melissa … I mean, Detective Ruiz."

"Hello, Detective," Jackson said excitedly; he hasn't had any time to calm down after his conversation with Keith. "I need to see you!"

"OK, slow down," Melissa said. "I'm calling because I talked to that waitress, Christine, and got a sketch drawn that I want you to look at."

"Yes! I also got some information!" Jackson said. "Can we meet now?"

"Yes. Detective Brown and I are at the police station if you wanna come and compare notes."

"I'll be there in fifteen minutes, Detective."

He had to sit down for a few minutes. Everything was coming at him. *Could the killer be Robert?* The murders had started around the same time he had started working. And he was there around the same time the two waitresses had been murdered. Jackson felt sad. He liked Robert a lot; he had trained him and had helped him get his job, and he trusted him. How could these two new people in his new life be connected? One was dead, and the other might be a murderer. He thought he should never have started a new life; he should have stayed right where he had been. Look where it had gotten him. Scarlet would be alive, and Robert would never have gotten through truck driving school let alone been hired at the same company if it hadn't been for Jackson.

He ran to the bathroom and threw up. He looks in the mirror; he looked pale and sick … with guilt. *Why's this happening to me?* He brushed his teeth, changed his shirt, grabbed his notes, and headed out. He was determined to get to the bottom of this.

He sat with the detectives at the station. "We meet again," Brown said as he got up and shook Jackson's hand.

"Have a seat," Ruiz said as she shook his hand. She wanted to make sure that from then on, she'd have Brown with her when she talked to Jackson. She couldn't help it; she was attracted to him, and she knew that was inappropriate.

"OK, Jackson, what you got for us?" Brown asked as they sat.

For some reason, Jackson didn't want to tell Brown anything; he liked talking to Ruiz. He felt comfortable with her. He turned to Ruiz. "You said you had a sketch of the young man Scarlet was talking with the day she was murdered."

Melissa turned to Jackson. She couldn't help being mesmerized by his eyes, how he looked at her. She could see why women were attracted to him. "Yes." She pulled a sketch out of a folder and slid it over to Jackson, who picked it up. It was as if his worst nightmare were coming true. It looked exactly like Robert. The pointy nose, the light-blue eyes, and his hair was short again. "Do you recognize this man?" she asked seeing the look of dread in Jackson's eyes.

Jackson put the sketch down. "I know this guy. I fuckin' know this guy! He's a truck driver, my friend." Jackson shook his head. "He's been a trucker for almost a year now."

"You're telling us you know this guy?" Brown asked.

"Are you sure?" Ruiz asked.

Jackson wanted to get it all out while it was still fresh in his mind. "I just found out that he was at both truck stops where Scarlet and the other waitress were killed."

Ruiz and Brown stared at Jackson; they couldn't believe what they were hearing. Brown jumped in excitedly. "You're telling us that the guy, this guy right here, is the killer? And on top of that, you know him, and he's your friend?" he asked raising his voice. He couldn't believe that with all the months he had worked on this case and all the people he had interviewed, this truck driver whom he'd met only twice had found out who the killer was. It was crazy.

"That's what I'm saying," Jackson said. "I knew something wasn't right with him the last two times I saw him even before Scarlet's murder. He just wasn't the same guy I had met, but I didn't think much of it until I started paying attention to these murders, and then Scarlet ..." Jackson paused and lowered his head; he felt like shit. "Then after her murder, I had to do something!"

Jackson told them about Robert having been a marine who had PTSD along with physical injuries and his weekly meetings and medications. The detectives needed as much information as they could before they interviewed Robert.

"Let us take it from here, Jackson," Brown said. "Go home, go back to your life, and let us do our job. I don't want you involved anymore in this case. You're way too connected to the victim and the suspect."

Jackson looked at Brown with disgust. *So now he finally wants to do his job!* All he wanted to do was go back to his room and lie down. He was in total disbelief about his life. "Please just get this motherfucker off the highway!"

He left the station and got to his pickup when he saw Ruiz running up to him. "Jackson, I'm so sorry about everything. We'll check him out thoroughly and see if all this information is correct. We might need you again," she said not wanting this to be the last time they saw each other.

"Maybe I can get a confession out of him," Jackson said. "I want to see him in person."

"I don't know about that. You need to not get any more involved."

"I'm already involved! Up to my fuckin' shoulders! I just want to do everything in my power to make it stop. I owe it to Scarlet and the others."

"You must have really loved Scarlet," Melissa said feeling jealous. She was developing feelings for this guy.

"Loved? I can't say I was in love with her, but I did care for her, and I know that if I hadn't been a coward, it could have maybe developed into love. The fact is that she loved me. She told me that the last night we were together, but I ran away. And now I'm back, and she's dead, and all I can think of is how she must have felt when I ghosted her like that. So please, Detective Ruiz, let me do what I can do to honor her."

Ruiz felt for him. She liked that he hadn't been in love with Scarlet. "I'll keep you posted and talk to my sergeant and Detective Brown about your helping us in California."

Jackson nodded. He got in his truck and took off. Back in his room, he turned on the TV, got the bottle of vodka he had in the fridge, and lay on his bed. He drank the rest of the day away.

Chapter 11

He woke up the next day feeling as if he were in an alternate universe. *How could all this bad, unbelievable shit be happening to me?* He decided to let it go for the time being, go home, back to work, back to the only things he still had in his life and let the detectives deal with the case. He believed that Ruiz would contact him if she needed something. Jackson wasn't blind; he knew Ruiz was attracted to him, and he was attracted to her, but he felt guilty about that because of his feelings for Scarlet.

He called Jim and told him he'd be available to drive as early as the next day. He also texted Ruiz telling her he'd be going back to California that day. Right after he texted her, she called him. "Hello," Jackson said.

"Hi, Jackson. This is Melissa, uh, Detective Ruiz. Thank you for all the information you gave us. We're going to California tomorrow to check out all the details. I can't tell you anything about it right now, but it's my day off today, and I'm here in Nevada, and I was wondering if you'd like to catch lunch before you head back. That's if you have any extra time, and lunch is on me. It's just a thank you for being so helpful." She didn't want to seem desperate.

"Yes, I'd like lunch," Jackson said knowing that it had taken a lot for her to ask him out; he had heard nervousness in her voice.

"Can you meet me in an hour at Sady's, the bar and grill right outside the city?" Melissa asked.

"Sure, I'll be there," said Jackson.

"See ya then," Melissa said finding herself blushing.

They got to the place at the same time. At first, he didn't recognize her; she was wearing her hair down, and she was in skinny jeans with a black tank top that showed off her shoulders and a small tattoo of a blue rose. He thought she looked hot. She had a small waist and a nice butt. She was sexy but not slutty.

She liked the way Jackson was looking at her up and down because she was doing the same thing. He was in his black Levi's and a white Vans T-shirt that showed off his biceps and the few tattoos he had on his right arm. He had some product in his short hair and was wearing his black and white Vans. Melissa was even more attracted to Jackson than she had thought she was, and she knew she might find herself in trouble that night.

They went in and ordered a couple of beers and some food and started talking. Jackson found himself comfortable with her. The fact that she was a detective made her even more attractive. He didn't understand why she had eyes for him; he felt she was way too good for him.

As they drank a little more, Melissa started feeling tipsy. "I know I'm breaking every rule in the book, Jackson, but I just had to see you alone. I know I'm probably freaking you out," she said hiding her pretty brown eyes, "but I'm attracted to you." She covered her face.

"No, not at all," Jackson said moving her hands away from her face. "I like that you called me and we're having lunch, but it's getting late, and I need to hit the road." What he really wanted to do was take her in his arms and have his way with her. He could tell that she wanted him, but it wasn't the right time. He saw her embarrassment at being rejected and didn't want her to feel like that. "Let's get this case solved, the killer behind bars, and give Scarlet and the others justice. I promise you that then," he said getting closer to her, "we'll explore whatever this is because I'm very much into you believe me," he said brushing her hair out of the way and kissing her lightly on the lips.

Melissa did feel embarrassed and rejected; she thought that she should never have said what she had said. "My fault. Sorry. I never should have invited you here. Very inappropriate of me," she said getting up.

"Wait," Jackson said as he pulled her back gently. "Don't feel bad or regret anything that happened here or anything you said. I'm glad you said it. It's just that it's not the time now," Jackson said again. He didn't want to make the same mistake he had with Scarlet with her or any other woman.

Melissa hugged him and looked at him. He was so beautiful in her eyes. "OK, but I'm still embarrassed. But yes, of course let's get this case solved. That should be our focus."

She started to apologize again, but he stopped her with a kiss and said, "Yes let's get this case behind us."

He walked her to her car. "See you soon, Melissa," he said and gave her another kiss.

Melissa just looked at him; that was the first time he had used her first name.

Jackson got home late; he was so tired from driving that he went straight to bed. The phone woke him up from a deep sleep. "Hello?"

"Jackson, where you been? Didn't you get my messages?"

It was Jim, and he was pissed, but Jackson wasn't the kind of guy anyone would want to get into a verbal confrontation with. "Hey! Slow the fuck down, and watch the way you talk to me!" He got off the bed pissed.

Jim stopped yelling; he was surprised and a little intimidated by the way Jackson had yelled back.

"Jim, sorry I didn't answer your phone calls, but I'm up now. If you have a load for me, I can be ready to drive in less than an hour."

"Yes, yes, I got something for you," Jim said in a calmer and softer voice that he wasn't used to using.

"Text me the when and where and I'll be there."

"I'll get it dispatched to you right now."

"Jim, next time, watch yourself and the way you talk to me," Jackson said in a rough but calm voice. "You hear me?"

"For sure, OK," Jim said, and they hung up.

Jackson hated being a badass. He had been one for many years and had gotten himself in trouble for not taking shit from anyone. He was afraid that due to what was happening, he'd become that guy again.

He showered and dressed; he looked at his phone for the dispatch, and he saw that Melissa had left a message. He felt a little something when her name popped up, but he also felt guilty for feeling that way because of the feelings he had for Scarlet. The text from Melissa said that she and Brown were going to talk to Jackson's supervisor that morning about Robert's routes for the last six months. The text ended with a simple, "I just wanted to give you a heads up."

Jackson didn't have time to read much into that text; he needed to get out the door and back on the road. He pulled up to the distribution center and saw his truck all clean and shiny with a trailer already attached. He had missed his truck, and he had missed driving. He needed it; it was the only thing he really had to look forward to.

Just when he was about ready to start the truck, Jim, Ruiz, and Brown walked over to him, and Jim had more than his usual serious look when he said, "Jackson these two detectives want to talk to you. Let's all go into my office."

"Don't I have a load I gotta drop off?" Jackson asked feeling a little annoyed; he hadn't known that he would be included in any of the questions right away, and he didn't want Jim or anyone else to know that he was the one who had pointed the detectives in Robert's direction.

"I got someone else to drop it off," Jim said.

Jackson was beyond annoyed; the look he gave Melissa made her nervous. Jackson wished Melissa had at least said something about this in her message.

They went into Jim's office and sat. Jackson took the chair that was closest to the door and crossed his arms. "So what's this all about?" he asked.

Brown turned to Jim. "Can I call you Jim?"

"That's my name. Go ahead. Let's get on with whatever this is," he said raising his arms.

"We need to see all the records on Robert Morris, any file you have on him, all the routes he's been on for the last six months," Ruiz said leaning in and trying to sound as professional as she could. But she was nervous; she didn't like the way Jackson was looking at her. She knew she should have given him more information in her text, but she had to be professional and act like a detective, not a friend.

"Why?" Jim asked. "What happened? What did he do?" He was beyond shocked. He didn't understand anything that was happening, and he didn't know why Jackson was there. His heart was racing. He was afraid he was going to have another heart attack; he had had one just over two years earlier. He took his medication that kept his heart in shape and looked back at the detectives.

"We have a court order here," Brown said handing it to Jim.

"Can you tell me what he's suspected of?" Jim asked feeling even more anxious.

"All we can tell you is that you need to ground him. We don't want him on any more routes until we come to a conclusion."

"What am I supposed to tell him?" Jim asked as he got on his computer to look up everything he had on Robert.

"You'll figure something out," Brown said.

The detectives seemed like they were done with the questioning when Jim printed out all the information. Jackson thought that they weren't going to ask him anything, but then Brown looked at him and asked, "So Jackson, is there anything else you need to tell us? Any more information about Robert? We just wanted to make sure you told us everything in Nevada."

Jackson was boiling with anger. They had called him out right in front of his boss, the last thing he wanted to happen, but he knew he needed to say something to get them out of there. "No, I told you everything then. I don't know why you pulled me in here. Didn't you tell me to leave it alone and let y'all do your jobs and for me to go back to my fuckin' life? Well, that's what I was trying to do when you guys basically pulled me off my truck!"

Jackson was beyond pissed and wasn't afraid to show it especially since this situation might have cost him his job.

"Hey! I can do whatever I need to do to get the answers I'm looking for!" Brown said trying to look intimidating, but Jackson wasn't at all intimidated.

"Y'all, let's just calm down. We're through here," Melissa said putting herself in between Jackson and Brown.

After they left, Jackson stayed. He knew that Jim was pissed and confused and needed answers.

"What in the holy fuck is going on?" Jim asked standing and glaring at Jackson.

Jackson didn't flinch. "Calm the fuck down! That's a free one, OK, Jim? You yell like that again at me and we're gonna have a serious problem."

Jim sat and in a calm voice asked, "Can you please tell me what's going on?"

Jackson told Jim everything and watched Jim's face turn pale and his eyes get wide.

"Excuse me," Jim said, and he ran to his restroom throwing up. When he came out, he said, "So you're saying Robert's a serial killer?"

"I'm just saying that that's a possibility. I had to tell the detectives what I knew."

"So what do I do about Robert? What do I say? How do I ground him from driving?" Jim asked sounding desperate.

"Just tell him that he's unable to drive right now because there was a complaint or something. When are you going to see him next?"

"Anytime now."

"Oh shit. OK, text him to come to the office first. When he comes out, I'll talk to him in private, maybe get some information from him. Don't tell him anything about what I know or that the cops came here asking about him. Soon enough, they'll approach him."

The two were trying to figure out what they were going to say to Robert.

"OK," Jim said after he texted Robert. "He's on his way."

"I'll be over by my truck acting like I just got back from somewhere. I'll talk to him, feel him out, see how he's doing."

Jim just nodded. He was trying to get himself together, but his heart was racing. He wasn't ready for another confrontation. He hoped that Robert would be cool about everything and that he could keep himself from being too nervous.

Jackson saw Robert pull up when he got in his truck. The trailer was gone; someone had taken his load. Robert was in Jim's office a good twenty minutes. When he walked out, he looked pissed and confused.

"Hey Robert!" Jackson yelled as Robert was walking toward his car. Robert turned around; the last person he had wanted to see was Jackson. All Jackson wanted to do was beat the living shit out of him, but he knew he couldn't. He needed to control himself and act like a friend. That was the only way Robert would trust him and hopefully let something slip out about the murders.

Chapter 12

"What's up?" Robert asked looking and acting nervous.

"Nothing much. What's up with you?" Jackson asked. "You don't look too good."

"I just got grounded. Can't drive for a while."

"Why? What happened?"

"I don't know, man," Robert said shaking his head. "Something about a complaint."

"Hey, come on," Jackson said putting a hand on Robert's shoulder. "Let's get a few beers and catch up."

Robert didn't have anything to do and at that point nowhere to go. "Why not?"

Jackson drove to Harry's, where they sat in the booth toward the back. After about three drinks and thirty minutes of small talk, Jackson finally started to ask questions. "So how's everything really, Robert? Are you taking care of yourself? Taking your meds and going to your meetings?"

"Why the fuck do you keep asking me that?" Robert asked raising his voice.

"Because I care about you! And to be honest, guy, you look like shit!"

That was true. Robert's hair was short, but it looked like he had cut it himself and had left a few small bald spots. He had been wearing the same clothes for like a week, and his eyes were bloodshot and had black circles from a lack of sleep.

"I'm good," Robert said feeling a bit tipsy.

"So why do you think they grounded you? You think it has anything to do with those murders?" Jackson asked realizing that it was time to get some answers.

"What the fuck you talking about?" Robert asked getting uneasy.

"I'm just asking," Jackson said feeling himself getting angry.

"You know what? I gotta get going," Robert said getting up and throwing down a twenty.

"Hey, hold up!" Jackson said throwing down another twenty and running after Robert. Robert looked extra nervous; his pupils were dilated, and he had his hands shoved into his pockets. "Let me take you back to your car," Jackson said as he calmed down.

Robert just stood there by the truck not wanting to get in. Jackson got in front of him. He couldn't hold back. He needed to press him while he had a chance. "You know they're saying that you're the serial killer!"

"What the fuck?" Robert said clenching his fist. "Who the fuck's saying that?"

"It all adds up. You were at the truck stops where two of the women were murdered, weren't you?" Jackson asked grabbing Robert by the collar of his jacket and pushing him against the wall in the alley they were parked in.

"Get the fuck off me, you psycho!" Robert yelled as he got out of Jackson's grasp and punched him in his face.

Jackson staggered back, got himself together, and tackled Robert to the ground putting his knee on his chest. "Just say it!" Jackson yelled wanting to slam his head on the ground.

"I wasn't at those truck stops!"

"Yes you were! I know you were! Stop fucking lying!"

"They were whores anyway!" Robert said.

Jackson let him up but pushed him up against the wall and punched him.

"I didn't do it! I didn't kill them whores!" Robert said as he was doubled over catching his breath. He stumbled and then threw up.

"You were in Nevada both times those waitresses were killed!"

Robert wiped the vomit off his face. Jackson wrestled him to the ground and pulled out his buck knife, which he held to Robert's neck.

"They were whores! They deserved it just like those nasty lot lizards!" Robert yelled as he felt the knife nick his neck.

"I knew one of those waitresses. She was my friend! She loved me! And you fuckin' killed her!" Jackson yelled pressing the knife even more to his neck drawing blood.

"What? You knew one of those whores? Which one? The one that drove the Kia or that cute little lady with the Nissan?"

At that moment, Jackson knew it; Robert had confessed. He wanted to slice his throat. Someone suddenly came out of the bar and yelled, "I called the cops! Get the fuck out of here!" Jackson dropped his knife, and Robert ran off. Jackson didn't try to stop him. He got in his truck and took off to his apartment. He was shaking. His suspicions were true. But he believed that Robert had killed just the waitresses, that there must have been another killer out there.

His mind was racing. His adrenaline was pumping. He couldn't believe that he had been right. But he didn't understand why a young man, a former marine, would do such a thing. What was Robert's motive? It seemed like he had this hatred toward prostitutes or maybe all women. He must have gotten the idea to murder them when he learned that someone out there was already killing women. He was a copycat killer.

Jackson called Melissa.

"Hello?"

"Melissa, this is Jackson. I need to see you! I talked to Robert just now, and he pretty much confessed to the last two murders. I don't think he was involved in the others," Jackson said talking a mile a minute.

"Slow down! We know he couldn't have killed all the women. He had alibis. We saw that on the route sheets. But yes, he was in the areas of the last murders. You said you talked to him about the murders?"

"I had to."

"No you didn't, Jackson! That's our job!"

Jackson knew she was pissed. "Melissa, I needed to! I thought you understood! Why did you call me to the office yesterday? That put all this other stuff in motion. I had to tell Jim about Robert also."

"Oh my God, Jackson! We were going to do all that tomorrow morning! Don't you understand? We have regulations we gotta abide by!"

"OK," Jackson said, "but I'm telling you, he knew about the vehicles the waitresses drove, so when you interview him, ask him about that!"

"I'll contact you when we get all the evidence in order. And Jackson, stay away from Robert!"

"You get that evidence you need and I will," Jackson said feeling annoyed with all the bullshit. "Please, Detective Ruiz, get these murders solved!" He hung up before she could say anything else.

Jackson woke up to the phone ringing again. It was Jim. "Oh my God, Jackson! They just arrested Robert!"

"Really? Good!" Jackson said sitting up in bed.

"No, it's not good at all! What's gonna happen when the public finds out we employed a fuckin' serial killer?"

"Jim, just be happy that he's behind bars."

"I know, I know. By the way, Jackson, I still have a business to run. Will you be available to drive today?"

"Sure," Jackson said feeling relieved but also sad that his friend had been arrested and concerned that there was another and more-brutal murderer out there.

He was getting ready to head out when someone knocked on his door. He opened it up and saw the two detectives.

"Can we come in?" Brown said. "We have a few questions."

"I'm running late for work," Jackson said. "I can give you only like ten minutes," he said looking at his phone.

They sat at the kitchen table. "We have Robert in custody," Brown said. "He tried to deny it, but he finally caved in to the two murders. He looked like he'd been worked over. Did you do that?"

"What did he say about that?" Jackson asked.

"He said he walked into a wall."

"Well then, there's your answer," Jackson said wondering why Robert hadn't said anything about their fight.

"We know that he was involved in the two murders," Melissa said, "but he denies the others, and he had alibis for those."

"So that means there's another monster out there!" Jackson said. "You have any leads on that person?"

"We just came here to inform you about Robert," Brown said. "Thanks for that major lead, but you need to let us do our job and stay out of it."

Jackson walked them out. He saw Melissa looking at him, so he gave her a smile; he didn't want her to think he was mad at her because he wasn't; he just needed to get his life back on track.

He drove to the distribution center and got in his truck, but then he sat there for a good ten minutes just thinking about everything. He felt bad for Robert. He knew something must have gone really wrong in his life for him to have done what he did. And he also felt for Scarlet, how she had been opening her heart again finally after what had happened in her past.

Jackson started up the truck, and he realized how much he had missed the sound of the engine, the vibration, and smell of the diesel. He felt at home there. He loved his job, and he was determined to be the best trucker he could be.

He rolled down the windows and headed for Nevada.

Chapter 13

The next couple of weeks went by slowly. Jackson tried keeping his mind off Scarlet and Robert, but it always drifted back to them. He had gone to court for Robert, who had pled guilty to two counts of second-degree murder. Jackson talked very little to Melissa; he felt that whatever there was between them was over. He couldn't help but think of the other murders; another victim had been found after Robert had been arrested.

Every night Jackson was at a truck stop, he kept his eyes out for anything shady. He slept only a few hours a day. He felt that he needed to get justice for the other women. He was obsessed with the case.

One cold, dark Sunday night, the stars were shining and the moon was full. He was sitting in his truck looking out the window when he saw an old, green, beat-up Volkswagen van pull into the truck stop. He kept his eyes on it as the headlights turned off. He saw a woman going over to it and talking to whomever was in the vehicle and then get in. *Oh my God!* He felt uneasy; he knew something was wrong. He jumped out of his truck and saw the van's headlights turn on; it slowly started pulling out of the truck stop. Jackson got close enough to get the license number. He wished he'd been able to stop the women from getting in the van. He went back to his truck and wrote down the license number; his adrenaline was pumping. He called Melissa even though it was two in the morning.

"Hello?" she answered in a sweet but sleepy voice.

"Melissa, it's Jackson. I have a license number for you! I saw this sketchy guy in a green Volkswagen van."

"Slow down," Melissa said as she got out of bed, trying to get herself together. "Did you say a green van?" Melissa's adrenaline was pumping.

"Yes I did."

"Oh my God! Give me the license number!" Melissa said, and Jackson did.

"Jackson, where are you?"

"At the Blue Bird truck stop outside Nevada."

"Stay there and stay calm. Detective Brown and I will be there first thing tomorrow morning."

"You think it's the guy?" Jackson asked excitedly.

"Don't know, but there were reports of a green van."

"I saw a women get in the van."

"I gotta go. I'll call you when we get close."

"Melissa, please get this guy!"

The next day, Jackson was physically and mentally drained. He had tossed and turned all night thinking of the guy in the van. He crawled out of his sleeper. He needed a shower and some coffee. As he was getting out of the shower, he saw two messages from Melissa saying that they would be there in forty-five minutes. He texted her back saying he'd be in the diner.

He was on his third cup of coffee when the detectives arrived. He felt a little nervous seeing Melissa again; he'd almost forgotten how pretty she was. She was wearing a light-pink blouse with black dress pants, and her hair was in a ponytail, which showed off her pretty face and light-brown eyes. She had on pink eyeshadow and matching pink lipstick. He couldn't stop looking at her as she walked in and sat next to him.

"What exactly did you see last night?" Brown said breaking up whatever was going on between Jackson and Melissa.

Jackson looked away from her to Brown, who was staring at him. "Didn't Melissa tell you?" Jackson said feeling a bit annoyed by Brown's question and by Brown himself. For some reason, he just felt judged by him.

"Yes she did, but I need to hear it from you on the record."

Jackson told them every detail he remembered. "Didn't you look up the license number?" he asked Melissa.

"Yes we did," Brown said cutting in. "It was an old registration. We have no idea who was driving it, but we have an APB out for the vehicle. Believe me, it shouldn't take that long before a highway patrol comes across the van."

"Unbelievable!" Jackson said. "So that means once again y'all can't do anything!" He was tired and cranky and fed up.

"Calm down!" Brown said. "We're doing the best we can."

"Bullshit you are! I'm the one looking out for anything and everything staying up not sleeping but maybe four hours a day on top of driving miles and miles and I'm able to come across this guy."

"We don't know if it's the guy," Brown said.

"Bullshit!" Jackson said. "Melissa told me you suspected that the killer drove a green Volkswagen van. You should have maybe said something about that to me so I could have been looking out for old Volkswagen vans! I'm the one doing your fuckin' job!"

Melissa didn't blame Jackson for being so pissed. "OK, Jackson, let's talk."

Jackson glared at both of them. "I'm done here! Go out and find this motherfucker! And don't contact me till you do!"

Jackson drove almost nonstop for the next three weeks with only a couple of days off here and there so he could catch up on his sleep. He called his sons; he needed to have someone steady in his life.

It was a warm spring morning. The sun was shining, and the traffic was light. For some reason, Jackson was in a good mood. He was heading home to take a few days off. He had plans to have his sons and their girlfriends over for dinner. His phone rang, and he heard Melissa's sweet voice. "Hello! How are you?" he said finding himself excited to be hearing from her. He had actually missed her and felt bad for the way he'd left things the last time he'd seen her.

"It's over!" Melissa said. "It's finally over! We have the man in custody. We arrested him last week. I didn't wanna call you till we were a hundred percent sure it was him."

"Oh my God! Really?" Jackson asked finding himself getting a little too excited and almost swerving into the other lane.

"Yes! He confessed to everything! I just wanted to let you know."

Jackson noted the nervousness in her voice. melissa liked him and felt something every time she saw or talked to him. "Thanks for calling. I'm so happy it's over! And I'm also sorry for how I reacted the last time we spoke."

"No big deal, Jackson. You were right. We should have done more. We really dropped the ball. If it weren't for you, we'd probably still be looking for the killer. Anyway, nice meeting you. I'll never forget you or this case."

"Nice meeting you too," Jackson said. "I just wish it had been under different circumstances."

They ended the call wishing each other good luck.

Jackson got back to the distribution center, parked, and unloaded his things. He was glad to be going home. When he got home, it was still early enough to invite the boys over for dinner. He just didn't want to be alone that night. He texted Josh and asked if he and Missy, his girlfriend, wanted to come over for dinner. "Sure! What time?" Josh texted back.

He also texted Jared the same question, but he was back in LA and wasn't able to come.

Jackson grilled some steaks, baked some potatoes, and prepared corn and salad. Josh and Missy arrived right when Jackson was setting the table. "Hi, Dad. How are you?" Josh asked giving Jackson a hug.

"I'm good," Jackson said.

"This is Missy, my one and only," Josh said as he pulled her close.

Missy was cute. Her hair was short and dyed blond, and she had four piercings in her ears and a tattoo of two lovebirds on her upper arm along with a few more tattoos on her forearm and a black rose tattooed on her right hand. She was not at all what Jackson had been expecting.

The dinner was good. They just chatted and laughed and didn't really say anything serious until Missy brought up the murders. "I heard you helped find the killers," she said looking at Jackson. "That's so awesome, man! Tell us all about it!" she said as she took her shoes off and sat cross-legged on the couch.

"No, Dad, you don't have to talk about it if you don't want to," Josh said giving Missy a look.

"You know what? It's OK," Jackson said actually feeling that he needed to talk about it to someone. He told them the whole story about Scarlet and Robert and even Melissa. Missy and Josh looked at Jackson in disbelief not interrupting once. Jackson finally finished and took a long swig of beer.

"Oh my God! That's fuckin' crazy, man! But at least they got the fucker!" Missy said as she got off the couch and headed to the bathroom.

"Are you really OK?" Josh asked; he saw sadness in his father's eyes.

"Yes, son, I'm fine now, but it was a lot to deal with."

They talked late into the night until Josh finally said, "We ought to be going. It's getting late."

Missy got her coat and gave Jackson a hug. "You really should call up that detective, Ruiz. I think you may have a crush on her," she said with a wink.

Jackson closed the door behind them. It was late. He was tired. He crawled into bed but with thoughts of Melissa entering his mind.

Chapter 14

Jackson woke up the next morning feeling rested, like a weight had been lifted off his shoulders. He was so relieved that the killer had been caught, and he had enjoyed the previous night with Josh and Missy. But there was something still weighing on his mind, something he couldn't shake off.

He showered, ate some breakfast, cleaned the kitchen from the night before, and sat in front of the TV to watch a game. He started looking at his phone and saw Melissa's name pop up. That's when he decided he wasn't going to let her go as he had Scarlet. He wasn't sure if she still had feelings for him, but he had them for her, and he had promised her that when all this was said and done and the killer was caught, he'd find her. It had been months since Scarlet had been murdered, and he realized he needed to put the past few months behind him and move on.

He texted Melissa saying that he needed to see her, that he wanted to talk about the killings. It was halfway true; he was curious who this fucker was and why he had committed the murders. But mostly, he wanted to talk about the two of them.

He went out to get a haircut, wash his truck, and handle a few more errands. He put on his blue Levi's, a button-up blue and grey plaid shirt, and his boots and drove the two hours to Fresno, where she was working a case.

It was a damp day. It had rained all night, and it was overcast and gloomy, but as soon as he reached Fresno, the sun started peeking out through the clouds. *Perfect*, he thought.

The two met at a diner. She was nervous but excited to see Jackson; she had never stopped thinking of him, and she hugged him when she saw him.

"Hello, Melissa," Jackson said while he checked her out. She looked beautiful. Her hair was down, and she was wearing skinny blue jeans, an off-the-shoulder maroon sweater, and black cowboy boots. "Are you off duty?" he asked as they sat at a cozy booth in the back.

"Yes I am," she said.

Jackson started talking first. "I wanted to apologize for being an asshole the last time I saw you. I'm not making any excuses, but I was cranky and tired. I need you to know that." He took her hand and gazed into her pretty brown eyes.

"You already apologized, Jackson. I'm the one who's sorry for not being a better detective. I'm embarrassed the way Detective Brown and I handled the case." Melissa looked away as tears filled her eyes. The case had been really hard on her to the point that she had almost quit. "Anyway," she said getting herself together, "The killer's name is Arnold Beets. He's a fifty-six-year-old man from Jean, Nevada, who had been living in his van for the last three years and surviving off his Social Security benefits."

"What was his motive? And if he'd been living for three years in his van, are there more than five victims?"

"We're not sure. He confessed to five. He said that they were evil and that they deserved to die. We found out that he had had mental health problems for years and that he had spent time in prison for assaulting his mother and her husband years ago. He's a total nut case. We're going to make sure he spends the rest of his life in prison."

Jackson felt that all that had happened to him and the people in his life had led him to where he was at this time and place. He took both of her hands. "Melissa, I don't know how you see me or even if you still like me, but I haven't stopped thinking about you since that first day I met you. I'm not perfect. I have my demons and some baggage, but I promised you that when this was all over, I'd find you. If you want to, we can see where this can go."

Jackson started to say more when Melissa got up and sat next to him and kissed him on the lips. "You had me at 'I haven't stopped thinking about you,'" she said, and they laughed.

From that day forward, they were a couple. Jackson continued to drive his big rig all over the West Coast, and Melissa was still a detective, but on her days off, she went with him.

Jackson never forgot about Scarlet or what may have been if these unforeseen circumstances hadn't happened. He didn't forget about Robert and how sick he must have been to do what he had done. How he wished none of it had happened, but it had, and it was something he'd have to live with for the rest of his life. But Jackson's life was good, and he was going to do everything in his power to keep it that way. Jackson would always remember Scarlet and the other victims murdered on what he called the Broken Highway.

Printed in the United States
by Baker & Taylor Publisher Services